A CHRISTMAS KISS

After Lord Crawton disappeared, Violet concentrated very hard on walking toward the stairs. With her candle still clutched in her hand, she turned once more toward the stairway.

To her horror, she was stopped once more.

This time, the gentleman was Mr. Halliday.

"Miss Leigh," he said, pulling her close to him. "I believe that we are under the kissing bough, so I am free to give you a kiss."

Violet looked up and saw it was true. She was under the kissing bough.

"You need not recoil, ma'am. I assure you that I realize you do not care for me, but tonight I take advantage of the holiday. And I noted that Lord Crawton did the same."

Here he pulled her close and kissed her. The warmth of his closeness and the intensity of his kiss shook her so deeply that she thought her knees might give way . . .

Books by Mona Gedney

A Lady of Fortune

The Easter Charade

A Valentine's Day Gambit

A Christmas Betrothal

A Scandalous Charade

A Dangerous Affair

A Lady of Quality

A Dangerous Arrangement

Merry's Christmas

Lady Diana's Daring Deed

Lady Hilary's Halloween

An Icy Affair

Frost Fair Fiancé

A Love Affair for Lizzie

The Affair at Greengage Manor

On the Twelfth Day of Christmas

Published by Zebra Books

ON THE TWELFTH DAY OF CHRISTMAS

MONA GEDNEY

ZEBRA BOOKS
Kensington Publishing Corp.
http://www.kensingtonbooks.com

ZEBRA BOOKS are published by

Kensington Publishing Corp.
850 Third Avenue
New York, NY 10022

All Kensington titles, imprints and distributed lines are available at special quantity discounts for bulk purchases for sales promotion, premiums, fund-raising, educational or institutional use.

Special book excerpts or customized printings can also be created to fit specific needs. For details, write or phone the office of the Kensington Special Sales Manager: Kensington Publishing Corp., 850 Third Avenue, New York, NY 10022. Attn. Special Sales Department. Phone: 1-800-221-2647.

First Printing: October 2004
10 9 8 7 6 5 4 3 2 1

Printed in the United States of America

CHAPTER 1

The morning room was filled with the hopeful sunlight following a spring rain, and Violet stood at the French windows that opened out upon the garden, watching a small squirrel busily rooting through a freshly-turned flower bed. He was, undoubtedly, searching for an acorn carefully hidden there last autumn. On a distant hill she could see the lacy froth of the cherry orchard, looking as dainty as one of Mama's gowns. Come July she would be able to wander through that orchard, admiring the ripe, red fruit and carrying some of it home in a pail to be baked in a tart for tea in the nursery.

Behind her, the pair of visiting aunts were busily plying their needles and chatting over their coffee. Violet ran her hand absently over the glossy lid of her mother's work cabinet, admiring once again the quaint Oriental scene etched in gilt upon its black-lacquered surface. She was allowed to open it and examine the little compartments within, filled with packets of needles, a rainbow of threads, and scissors with gilt handles. She was about to avail herself of this privilege when she suddenly focused on what the aunts were saying. The words stabbed her as sharply as ever the little sewing scissors had.

"It is a thousand pities that the child has none of her mother's beauty or charm."

Great-Aunt Matilda held up her scissors glasses and eyed Violet appraisingly after this pronouncement. "She is the image of her father, and will probably be quite as tall. It is most unfortunate that what is acceptable in a man can spell doom to a female, but that is the way of the world."

Matilda was her mother's widowed aunt. Matilda and her sister, Agatha, came once every year or so to visit their niece and her family. Matilda was fond of terrorizing her relatives and delivering her judgments of them, their lives, and their futures, untroubled by any sense of delicacy. She was, she said, an advocate of honest speaking at any price. She was, naturally, less inclined to hear it than to speak it.

"Still," Matilda added, returning to her work with the satisfied air of someone who has just come upon a crumb of comfort, "she will be of some use to the family. She will be able to care for her parents in their declining years, and certainly she can look after her nieces and nephews, for Adrian and Cynthia will undoubtedly marry. Violet will have the satisfaction of being of service to her family."

Great-Aunt Agatha, Matilda's spinster sister, had risen quickly from her tambour frame as soon as Matilda had begun her unhappy assessment of Violet's future. She hurried over to the child, taking her hand and leading her out onto the stone terrace that overlooked the garden.

"You mustn't mind Matilda," she said, looking down at Violet, her tissue-thin skin folding into a fine network of wrinkles as she smiled. "She believes that everyone wants to hear precisely what she is thinking—whether it is true or not."

Violet shook her head sadly. "But what she said *is* true, Aunt. I know that I'm not beautiful like Mama—or like Adrian and Cynthia."

Even at the age of ten, Violet was aware of the great abyss that yawned between her and her mother, who was fine-boned and delicate, golden and laughter-filled. Mama's every move was graceful, while Violet recognized that she herself was awkward and bony, her dark eyes too large for her face, her feet too large for her body—quite unlike her younger brother and sister, who were miniatures of their mother. Nonetheless, even though she saw the truth of Great-Aunt Matilda's observations, hearing someone else comment upon her deficiencies was painful.

"Adrian and Cynthia are going to be just like Mama," she added with a sigh. Even though she loved her younger brother and sister, it seemed unfair that they should already be universally admired for their beauty. Everyone, from Nurse to the rector, commented upon it. Violet was considered sweet-natured, but, judged simply upon their appearance, the younger pair were dubbed angelic by all who encountered them. Their sister was scarcely noted. Violet would have traded her own sweet nature for just a thimbleful of their beauty.

"I expect that they will be," conceded her aunt fairly, "but you have an advantage that they will never have."

Violet looked at her hopefully. She could not for a moment imagine what she might have that Adrian and Cynthia did not already possess.

"Your brother and sister do not have to determine what their personal resources are," continued Agatha. "They will be able to trade upon their beauty when they deal with others, so they may never have the slightest notion of what other gifts they may have. You, on the other hand, will have to depend upon yourself, my girl, so you must come to know what your resources are."

Violet looked at her aunt uncertainly. So far as she could see, she was quite well acquainted with her resources. Her glass offered a painfully clear picture.

"I don't believe I have any, Aunt."

Agatha chuckled. "Of course you do, my dear. I've watched you carefully. You are kind-hearted and clever, which is a most unusual combination. Those two advantages alone will set you apart from many, and will make you good company for yourself, which is a more important consideration than many people realize."

A long minute passed while Violet thought this over, then she shook her head. "I'd rather be pretty."

Great-Aunt Agatha laughed again and patted her hand. "So would we all," she agreed. "It makes things ever so much easier. Unfortunately—or perhaps fortunately—we must play the hand we are dealt."

Violet was familiar with that expression, for she was already an expert card player. Papa had taught her to play Beggar My Neighbor and then Casino and Commerce as well. "And so it is just chance that made me plain and Cynthia pretty? Just as it is chance that decides which cards we're dealt in a game?"

"Some would say so," conceded her aunt. "But chance has nothing to do with how we play those cards. Not if we use the wits God gave us."

Violet nodded thoughtfully. She understood that. One had to be alert when playing a card game, and when there were options, careful consideration had to be given to the possible consequences of each.

As she grew older, she came to appreciate the wisdom of Agatha's advice. She understood that the marriage portions allotted to her and to Cynthia were too small to tempt suitors, although Cynthia's face was her fortune and she had had a string of admirers from the time she was in the cradle. No one doubted that she would marry well.

When Violet went away to Miss Delaware's Seminary for Young Ladies, she had learned to make her way in a wider world than her home. Although she was certainly still not a beauty, her appearance was distinctive, for she did not attempt to minimize her height, either by her carriage or by her choice of dress or hairstyle. Instead, she stood even straighter and chose her gowns to emphasize her height.

Indeed, Delight Ashton, one of the other young ladies at the seminary, had informed her on one occasion that she looked for all the world like a may-pole and had suggested that the rest of the girls dance about her on May Day.

"You are just right for the part," she had remarked, laughing and twirling about Violet, looking up at her to emphasize the great difference in their heights, for Delight was small and dainty.

Violet was accustomed to her jabs, however, and replied in a pleasant, easy manner. "I would be happy to serve as the may-pole if you like, but only upon the condition that you deck me with mayflowers and scarlet ribbons. I should not wish to be thought an unfashionable may-pole."

The other girls had laughed and Delight, irritated by their amusement and by the fact that Violet, though no beauty, was admired for her style, had flounced from the room.

Violet had more than one occasion to be thankful for the advice of her great-aunt. She had taken stock of her resources, as Agatha had told her to, and gradually grown more comfortable with herself and more confident in her ability to look after herself and her family. Her father was always her staunch ally, but they had lost him when she was fifteen. She discovered then that someone must be the sensible, steady member of the household, and appointed herself to that role.

It was, she quickly discovered, a much more difficult undertaking than she could have imagined.

CHAPTER 2

"Here comes that old court card Needley. I daresay it will take his footman and half-dozen others to prise him from that antique carriage of his. The old bag-pudding has gotten as fat as a flawn, but he is still tricked out in his knee breeches and peacock colors and patches. His valet must suffer the deepest mortification to see his master go abroad in such a costume!"

Percival Fitzroy, secure in the knowledge that he was the pride and joy of his own valet, allowed himself a delicate shudder. The bow window of White's afforded an excellent view of those arriving at the club and those passing along St. James Street, and Fitzroy assessed them all carefully, offering his commentary in a running monologue.

Travis Halliday leaned back comfortably in his well-upholstered chair and closed his eyes, but he could not close out the biting comments of his companion, who continued to scrutinize all passers-by through his quizzing glass and to share his observations. Fitzroy was a quick-witted, critical man, devoted to all things fashionable, while Halliday was a notable sportsman and gamester. A more unlikely pair of friends could scarcely be found, but friends they had been since their school days, when Halliday had soundly trounced a bully who had been tormenting the younger, frailer Fitzroy. He frequently reminded Fitzroy of the episode, lamenting that his decision to intercede had been a regrettable one and that he should have abandoned Fitzroy to his fate, an observation that perturbed his dapper friend not in the least.

"And there is Lumley, thinking himself at home to a peg when all the world knows he ain't. That pair of nags he's driving are gypsy goods if ever I've seen any. They'll be off to the knacker in no time."

Fitzroy adjusted his glass disapprovingly and leaned closer to the window to observe this new offender. "And his neckcloth looks as though the stable boy gave him a hand with it, and his coat has so much padding he looks like a pigeon. I'd give a plum to see Brummell look him up and down. Lumley would stop thinking himself such a fine fellow in very short order."

Fitzroy allowed himself a moment of satisfaction as he thought of the hours it had taken his own valet to arrange his cravat in a flawless Waterfall and to fit him into his perfectly tailored coat of blue superfine, which fit like a second skin. Although his dressing ritual was neither so long nor so elaborate as that of Brummell, he felt that the results were not to be despised.

"You have gotten so high in the instep, Fitzroy, that soon you will speak to no one save yourself and God—and to the Beau, of course." Halliday's eyes were still closed, so he was unable to appreciate Lumley's sartorial disaster. "I wonder that you allow yourself to be seen with me."

There was a pause while Fitzroy turned his glass upon his friend and assessed him carefully, then let the quizzing glass fall so that it dangled from its black satin ribbon.

"You could have a point there, Hal," he replied agreeably. "I believe I see a small crease in the sleeve of your coat and I am certain that *your* boots were not blacked with champagne."

Halliday opened one eye and regarded his maligned boots for a moment, then studied the mirror-bright perfection of Fitzroy's. Then he sighed, closed the eye, and sank once more into the welcoming depths of his chair. European visitors to England made much of the comfort of the chairs, made for such easy lounging and not for sitting bolt upright.

"You unman me, Fitzroy. I can see there is nothing for it but to let Vincent go. I shall inform him tonight that his services are no longer required."

"Most amusing! Pray spare me your barbed wit," retorted Fitzroy. "I am well aware that you think that I carry things to extremes, but it would do no harm for Vincent to take a little advice from my man."

When Halliday, who now appeared to have sunk into a gentle slumber, did not respond, Fitzroy eyed him with discontent. Despite the superiority of his boots and the artistic arrangement of his cravat, he was keenly aware that Halliday appeared to greater advantage in his clothes. Weston, that tailor without peer, was compelled to add a little padding to the shoulders of Fitzroy's coats, while Halliday required none at all. Nor did Halliday spend hours striving for perfection with his neckcloth, yet he still achieved an easy and enviable elegance. Even Beau

Brummell himself, the *ton*'s final word on all things fashionable, had remarked upon it.

Fitzroy's attention was suddenly attracted to the street once more and he sat up abruptly, quivering in the same intent, keen-eyed manner of a terrier that has scented a rat.

"Good Lord, it's Crawton! I can't believe he has the *effrontery* to show his face in town, but there he is, just as cool as a cucumber!"

"What's amiss with Crawton?" inquired Halliday, neither moving nor opening his eyes. "Is his cravat crooked?"

"I knew that you weren't asleep!" Fitzroy informed him triumphantly. "As to Crawton, everyone knows that he was caught fuzzing the cards not more than a fortnight ago. He was at a private party, and he had almost left young Cranston without a feather to fly with before he was detected. Limmer was the host, and he tried to keep the unsavory matter a secret, but naturally it was widely known by the next morning."

Gossip was the life-blood of the *ton*, and Percival Fitzroy did his part to keep that life-blood flowing.

"I daresay Cranston will think twice before he allows himself to be taken in again," remarked Halliday, yawning. "So long as he didn't actually take the boy's money, Crawton may have taught him a valuable lesson."

His companion, annoyed that Halliday did not fully appreciate the enormity of Crawton's offense, snorted his dismissal of such a ridiculous notion. "And we know how well you learned your lesson, Hal! Near disaster has not kept you from the gaming tables!"

"Very true, but at least I am never cheated. When I lose, I lose to an honest man—and I never risk everything."

Fitzroy paid him no mind, having returned his attention to the window once more.

"And now just look at him!" he said in disgust. "Strutting in here as pretty as you please! And we're supposed to sit down to dinner in a club that allows a Captain Sharp among its membership."

Halliday, deciding that he had endured quite enough and that a change of scene was desirable, rose from his chair immediately.

"Then we will assuredly not do so, Fitzroy. I have no objection at all to having our dinner elsewhere. Since I know you have no engagement until the Emerson ball, we may dine at our leisure."

"And so you are not deigning to favor us with your presence at the ball? What a surprise that is!"

"As you well know, I have no taste for dancing with simpering young women, Fitz. And the penny stakes in the card room of a ball are scarcely of interest, either."

"Still, you *could* come just for a few minutes. It would not be so very painful a sacrifice."

When Halliday did not reply, he pressed his point. "Why not give up your gaming for one evening, Hal? Your appearance would be quite a feather in Mrs. Emerson's bonnet. Not so good as persuading Brummell to attend, of course . . . but, still, it would be quite impressive to have you leave the faro table for her ballroom."

Eager to avoid the despised Crawton, who had not yet made his appearance upstairs, Fitzroy rose with alacrity and headed for the door. Halliday followed him at a more leisurely pace but, to Fitzroy's relief, they managed to secure their hats and walking sticks and make their way undetected to the safety of the street.

"Crawton must be informed that he is no longer welcome at the club," Fitzroy announced firmly. "I shall look into the matter tomorrow."

"I wouldn't do so if were you, Fitz," observed Halliday idly. "If White's were to tell everyone touched by scandal broth that he was no longer welcome, we should have very few members left. Most of us have a skeleton or two that we would prefer remain hidden."

"Yes, but that's just it! Crawton's *isn't* hidden! *Everyone* knows about it—except for you, of course, and you *would* know if you spent any time in polite society instead of with the dice box or tossing down daffy with your sporting friends! Crawton is a shameless sneaksby: a cardsharp, the lowest of all low creatures!"

"But it isn't as though the problem arose at White's or at Brooks's, Fitz. If Limmer won't say it's true, and undoubtedly Cranston won't want to admit it, you will go nowhere with this. Be reasonable. You have only hearsay to rely upon, and you will create a storm for nothing. Although I admit that I am no fan of Crawton, I think you should let the matter lie."

Fitzroy looked unconvinced, so Halliday persevered. His friend was strongly inclined to act upon impulse and regret his actions later.

"You know that the *ton* is filled with gamblers, Fitz. When I very nearly managed to lose the whole of my fortune in a single evening, I became the subject of drawing room gossip myself for at least a day or two."

"Well, of course you were—and I admit I don't understand for an instant why you continue to gamble after such a near disaster—but you and Crawton are worlds apart! Your two situations cannot be compared at all! You are two very different kinds of men!"

Halliday shrugged. "It appears to me that we have much in common, little though I like the man. We are both confirmed gamesters."

Fitzroy shook his head so vehemently that his tall beaver hat almost flew off his head.

"What you do is not the same thing at all, Hal, as you very well know! A gentleman may indeed lose everything he owns at the gaming table without being any less a gentleman!" he protested. "Besides, you won it all back the next night . . . and *you* don't cheat!"

Among the members of the *ton*, few things were regarded with more disdain than cheating at cards or failing to pay a debt of honor acquired at the gaming table. One might, naturally, go for years without paying the bills from one's tailor or jeweler or milliner, but, in the view of those that mattered, such things had nothing to do with honor.

Fitzroy, certain of his ground, was preparing to enlarge upon his subject when a sudden force catapulted into him from behind, sending him headlong to the pavement in a tangle of legs and boots.

Before Halliday could move to extricate his friend, another figure bore down upon them and pulled at one of the boots waving in the air.

"Oh, Adrian, you *cawker*! How came you to do such a thing! Are you hurt?" This question came from a young girl, breathless from running and with her chip bonnet askew over bright curls and blue eyes. She was, Halliday thought with appreciation, an exact replica of one of the dainty shepherdesses much admired in romantic paintings. However, she was just as clearly a girl still in the schoolroom, whose language and manner were decidedly neither dainty nor romantic.

Before the individual thus addressed could reply, however, the vision dissolved into laughter. "What a cake you have made of yourself!"

"I believe we can safely say, Cynthia, that we all three of us have made spectacles of ourselves, and this poor gentleman is our victim."

Halliday looked up to see that the speaker was a tall young woman in a well-cut, dark walking dress, who was moving swiftly toward them without quite breaking into a run. Violet had viewed the accident from a distance, and was hoping against hope that the gentleman who had been run down had not sustained any lasting damage. Chaperoning her brother and sister always presented a challenge, even at home, but here in London there were far too many opportunities for them to get into trouble. She and her mother had been in London for a few weeks, this being the time of Violet's coming-out, and Adrian and Cynthia had joined them only two days earlier. *Two eventful days earlier*, Violet thought grimly.

Halliday turned back to help the dazed Fitzroy to his feet. He was a pitiable sight, his neat, biscuit-colored breeches ripped at the knee, his cravat a wreck, and his glossy boots scuffed. The boy who had run him down sprang up lightly, his face crimson, and hurried to restore Fitzroy's hat and walking stick, both of which had gone flying at the moment of impact. He was, Halliday noted with interest, the male counterpart of the shepherdess, quite as striking in his golden good looks. The young woman with them, he surmised by her dress and demeanor, was their governess.

"I am very sorry, sir," said the boy. "I hadn't meant to plow into you like that, but truly I didn't see you. I was looking up there." Here he indicated a narrow-railed balcony on the building just beyond them.

"There he is, Adrian! There he is!" shrieked Cynthia, pointing with her parasol and jumping up and down. "There's Jocko! Don't let him get away again!"

"Cynthia, do try for a little conduct, my dear," remonstrated Violet in a low voice. "Remember that you are in public now."

Cynthia made a visible effort to control herself, her eyes still glued on the monkey, and, with an apologetic glance at Fitzroy, the boy turned away and hurried in the direction of a small, dark monkey swinging casually from the railing of the balcony.

"Indeed we are so *very* sorry, sir," said Violet, turning from her charges to their victim. "Pray allow us to call our carriage and take you to your home so that—"

Here she broke off and put her gloved hand to her mouth in dismay. "Why, Mr. Fitzroy! I had not realized that it was you!"

"Miss Leigh!" gasped Fitzroy, hearing his name and finally able to focus clearly upon the scene. Seeing her, however, his sense of propriety returned to him in full force. "Whatever are you doing here on St. James Street, Miss Leigh? You should not be seen here, you know."

St. James Street, home to several exclusive clubs for gentlemen, was tacitly considered off-limits to well-bred young females. Only a hoyden would allow herself to be subjected to the curious gaze of those watching from the windows of Boodle's, Brooks's, and White's. He glanced from her startled face to the windows above him, and both of them flushed at the sight of the interested viewers ranged there. Fitzroy noted unhappily that they had also managed to draw a small crowd of onlookers around them on the street. Two or three carriages and a handsome curricle had also paused to take stock of the excitement. He would, he had no doubt, be regaled with stories of his disaster for weeks to come.

"Yes, I know that, sir, but I am afraid my brother and sister left me little choice," she replied, with what Halliday considered admirable composure, given the circumstances. "Just as we came out of Bullock's Museum, Adrian's monkey broke away from him and ran around the corner. My sister followed them, so naturally I had no choice but to come down this street, too."

"Naturally," agreed Mr. Halliday amiably, having followed this exchange with amusement. "You cannot have Jocko racing about London unchaperoned."

"Forgive me, Miss Leigh," said Fitzroy, regaining enough of his own composure to remember his manners. "Allow me to present my friend, Mr. Travis Halliday."

Halliday returned her brief curtsey with a bow, reassessing her identity and noting with appreciation that she carried herself well and that the severity of her dark gown suited her, serving to underscore her fine complexion and willowy height. And he was pleased to see that even being part of a party including two hey-go-mad youngsters and a monkey had not overset her.

"Miss Leigh is the elder daughter of Mrs. Anthony Leigh of Richland," he added.

"Indeed?" replied Halliday, his attention fully caught. "I knew your father, Miss Leigh. I had the pleasure of sitting down to a game of whist with him a good many evenings when he was in town. He is greatly missed."

"Thank you, sir." Violet's eyes grew bright with unshed tears, but she managed a smile. Even though her father had been dead for more than two years, she had never quite made her peace with his absence.

"And I am acquainted with your mother as well, of course," said Halliday. "I hope that she is well."

Fitzroy opened his mouth to add something, but any further exchange was prevented for the moment. A cry from Cynthia was echoed by that of the gathering crowd, and Violet turned anxiously toward Adrian and Jocko. The monkey had discovered that he could ascend to the upper floors of the building and, ignoring Adrian's attempts to coax him down, was making his way with great dexterity toward the roof.

"Does Jocko usually accompany you on your outings in town?" inquired Halliday with a smile.

"Naturally not," Violet replied briskly. "My mother had asked Mr. Bullock to procure a monkey for Adrian, and he was kind enough to do so. We had just stopped at his museum to get Jocko." If she had her own reservations about the wisdom of her mother's request, she did not allow them to show.

"And was there no cage for Jocko?" inquired Halliday curiously, watching the monkey's antics in the distance.

She flushed more deeply and nodded her head. "Yes, but I'm afraid that my sister opened it before I could stop her. She cannot bear to see animals restrained in any way."

Halliday glanced up at Jocko, who was now dangling casually from a fourth-story window and watching those below him with interest. Their gasps and the loud advice of one young gentleman for everyone to stand back so that the creature wouldn't harm anyone when he fell served to convince the monkey that he was now the center of attention.

The monkey clearly had a well-developed sense of theater. Recognizing that he had an admiring audience below him, he pulled himself onto the window sill, where a pot of bright flowers resided. He carefully plucked one of the geraniums and placed it daintily between his teeth, grinning down at his admirers. There was a spatter of applause, which seemed to spur Jocko to further action. He took the flower and waved it gently in the air, then tossed it to the group below, quite in the manner of famous actresses favoring their audiences. Laughter followed and one of the gentlemen retrieved the flower and tucked it into his lapel.

"Isn't Jocko cunning?" crowed Cynthia, clapping her hands as she watched his performance.

"Cunning?" demanded Fitzroy, restored enough that he was able to raise his quizzing glass to his eye once more and look at her in disbelief. Turning to Halliday, he added, "The creature should be sent by post down to Oatlands. I daresay the Duchess wouldn't even notice one more."

The Duchess of York, a most eccentric but well-liked lady, kept her own private menagerie at her estate. Guests were compelled to make their way among droves of dogs, monkeys, parrots, macaws, and the occasional kangaroo. Fitzroy had barely survived the honor of an invitation to a house party there, and had carefully avoided any further visits. He could not expose himself or his wardrobe to such an experience again.

"I believe that Jocko would not wish to be part of an ensemble," observed Halliday, still watching the monkey. "He appears to prefer solo performances."

"I'm going into the building, Vi," called Adrian, turning toward his sister. "He's never going to come down here just because I am calling him, but I might be able to persuade him to come to me if I can get behind him in the window."

"He'll be gone before you ever get there," replied Halliday. "He's already set his sights on the roof."

Adrian looked up and saw with dismay that Halliday was correct. Jocko had swung to the top of the window and was carefully picking his way upward.

Halliday glanced at Fitzroy's quizzing glass, rimmed in gold, glinting brightly in the afternoon sun. It hung securely on a black satin ribbon worn around his neck.

"Just the thing," he said, slipping the ribbon over his friend's head. "This will bring him down."

Before the outraged Fitzroy could react, Halliday had taken it over to Adrian and handed it to him.

"Call to him again and swing this so that it catches the sun," Halliday instructed him. The boy took the glass gratefully, eager to try anything to prevent the monkey from disappearing across the rooftops.

"Jocko!" he called. "Look here!"

"Just as though the little beast is going to recognize his name!" observed Fitzroy bitterly. Then, in astonishment, he saw the monkey pause and look down.

"Of course he knows his name," replied Cynthia indignantly. "Mr. Bullock says that he has always been called that—and Jocko is a very intelligent animal."

The quizzing glass had caught Jocko's attention and, after studying it attentively as Adrian waved it in the sunlight, he began climbing swiftly back toward the street, chattering loudly. The crowd murmured appreciatively, and then broke into laughter as Jocko swung into the boy's arms and took the glass from him. Carefully the monkey slipped the ribbon over his own head and then lifted the glass to his eye and turned toward the crowd.

"Quite the gent," observed one man. "He can look down his nose at us with the best of them!"

"It's completely ruined!" said Fitzroy bitterly. "I hope that this satisfies you, Hal. I purchased that glass specially at Rundell and Bridge! There is not another one like it!"

"Well, you must at least grant that Jocko has excellent taste," replied Halliday, quite unmoved. "I shall order you another . . . although I feel that you would do just as well without one."

Violet, who had hurried over to the rescued pet with her sister, had missed this unhappy exchange. Having assured herself that this time her brother had a firm grip on Jocko, she returned, smiling, at Fitzroy and Halliday.

"How very kind you both are! As soon as we can coax Jocko back into his cage, Adrian will bring your glass back to you, Mr. Fitzroy. It shall take no more than two minutes, I promise you."

"Oh, that won't be at all necessary!" answered Fitzroy hastily, trying to repress a shudder at the thought of wearing the same ribbon and using the same glass as Jocko. "Consider it a gift, dear lady!"

"A gift!" she replied, astonished. "But I cannot possibly do so, Mr. Fitzroy. Why, that is clearly an expensive piece; not simply a pretty trinket!"

Every inch the gentleman, Fitzroy did not allow himself a sidelong glance at his friend, who was following the exchange with amusement.

"Nonsense," Fitzroy responded firmly, quite as though he had voluntarily parted with his beloved glass. "In an emergency, one must do whatever is necessary."

Violet smiled at him warmly. "Well, it is very kind, and we are all most grateful to you."

"And to you, sir," she added, turning to Halliday. "You were very quick off the mark. Another moment or two and Jocko would have been lost to us."

He bowed briefly. "Well, we certainly could not have that. I should hate to think of your not having the pleasure of Jocko's company—and monkeys live for many years, I understand. I daresay he will still be with you some twenty years from now, enjoying every family celebration."

Her face fell slightly at this oppressive thought, but she managed to maintain her smile while gathering her charges.

"Shall I see you at Mrs. Emerson's ball tonight, Miss Leigh?" Fitzroy inquired, hoping to divert her thoughts to happier topics.

She smiled at him and nodded, reaching over to straighten Cynthia's bonnet.

"Then I shall look forward to standing up with you there, ma'am. Pray reserve a dance for me."

"That is the least that I can do, Mr. Fitzroy, after your gallant contribution to Jocko's welfare . . . and your great restraint in not turning us all over to a magistrate for assault," she replied, laughing. "I was afraid that you would wish never to see me again."

"Nonsense!" protested Fitzroy stoutly, ignoring his rapidly-stiffening knee and the wreckage of his wardrobe. He carefully averted his eyes from Jocko so that he would not be forced to see his prized glass in small, barbaric paws. "Dancing with you is always a pleasure, ma'am."

The two men watched until she had herded her small flock safely around the corner and onto Piccadilly.

"That was really most unkind of you, Hal," said Fitzroy, frowning at his friend.

"What was?" he asked absently. "Giving Jocko your glass?"

"Naturally, *that* was unkind—but I meant what you said about the life span of that reprehensible little animal. I don't believe Miss Leigh is looking forward to spending years in Jocko's company any more than you or I would be."

"Rather less, I should imagine," agreed Halliday. "But I would guess that so long as her brother and sister insist upon it, Jocko will have a home with them. And when they go their separate ways, Miss

Leigh will probably feel honor-bound to provide Jocko with a home."

"I shall expect you to order me a new glass immediately, Hal." Fitzroy's voice was firm as his thoughts dwelt once more on the wrong that had been done him. "I feel quite lost without it."

Halliday was still watching the corner, but he turned back at that. "How will you manage without it at the ball tonight?" he asked lightly. "Who will know they have come under your disapproving—or admiring—eye if you are not quizzing them with it?"

"I shall manage well enough," he responded stiffly. "I must say, though, that it is quite shocking to discover that Miss Leigh's brother and sister are so wild in their ways. Their mother, of course, has always been a flirt, I understand, but with a sense of delicacy—and *Miss* Leigh is very much a lady, very well-bred."

"I did not realize that you knew Miss Leigh so well, Fitz. I had not heard you mention her." Halliday scrutinized him a moment. "Have you a *tendre* for the young lady?"

"Not at all . . . and I *don't* know her well. But, after all, this is her first season and one *can* be kind, Hal, particularly to the daughter of Marianne Leigh. I met her at Almack's a fortnight or so ago. She is a very gracious young woman, and her mother, of course, has always been considered enchanting, and a great beauty as well."

He thought about that for a moment. "The younger sister promises to be a diamond of the first water, too, although somewhat wild just yet. It is a pity that Miss Leigh has none of their beauty."

Halliday shrugged. "She is distinctive, though.

Quite attractive, in fact. And there is certainly nothing missish about her."

Fitzroy looked up sharply at this and decided to press his advantage. "Perhaps you might join us at Mrs. Emerson's tonight, Hal," he remarked, keeping his voice casual.

Halliday's reply was equally casual. "Perhaps I might, Fitz. Perhaps I might."

He paused and appeared to sink deeply into thought, then added, "Although the absence of Jocko must be felt, of course. Were he there, Fitz, he might lend you his glass."

CHAPTER 3

Daisy Emerson's ball was considered a great success by those in attendance, for the crush was so great that the guests could scarcely move, and no hostess could hope for a higher accolade. The carriages bearing them there had so clogged Mount Street that the wait to reach the front door could be as great as half an hour.

"It appears as though we will need a bootjack to gain entrance," complained Halliday as he and Fitzroy looked at the throng gathered there. "Perhaps we should go elsewhere this evening."

"Nonsense!" replied Fitzroy briskly, happy to have gotten his friend thus far. He had been trying for months to entice Halliday away from the gambling halls and green rooms of the theaters back into what he considered a more civilized society. "We will be inside in no time at all, and then you will be pleased that you have come."

Halliday looked distinctly doubtful about this pronouncement, but Fitzroy kept him engaged in conversation until they were safely on the stairway leading to the first floor, with so many people behind them that a hasty exit was no longer an option. At that point, Fitzroy decided that he could indulge his curiosity. Halliday's unexpected reversal of his position about attending this ball demanded some explanation.

"How is it, Hal," he began casually, "that you decided to come tonight after all?"

Noting his friend's lifted eyebrows, he added hastily, "Of course I'm delighted that you did . . . and Mrs. Emerson will be quite overcome when she sees you."

Halliday's tone, when he replied, was one of patience tried to the extremity. "I have come, naturally, to dance, Fitzroy. That is, I believe, what one does at a ball—except, of course, when there is no space left in which to stand up." Here he glanced about him with distaste.

"I thought perhaps you had come to play cards." Fitzroy knew well the answer to this comment, but he had craftily decided to disguise his real question in the midst of a covey of others.

"I have brought a pocketful of farthings especially for that very thing," replied Halliday agreeably. "White's and Brooks's will have nothing to compare with the game I shall strike up with the dowagers and retired colonels in the card room. I daresay I shall emerge very plump in the pocket by the end of the evening and shall spend the whole of my winnings on a bag of hot chestnuts in the park tomorrow."

Fitzroy disregarded Halliday's sarcasm and smoothed the impeccable sleeve of his dark evening coat with satisfaction. His had been a grueling day. When he had arrived home, his valet had almost taken to his own bed upon seeing the wreckage of his master's clothing. Nevertheless, after Fitzroy had recruited his strength with a brandy and a brief nap and a poultice for his knee, he was able to submit himself once more to the ministrations of the inimitable Briggs. The result, they felt, was worthy of them both, and he had sallied forth with confidence to greet the world once more, while Briggs prepared to address his efforts to the restoration of Fitzroy's abused boots.

"It is possible, too, that you have come because your conscience is troubling you," remarked Fitzroy idly, sighting a miniscule speck on his sleeve and removing it fastidiously.

"On the contrary, my conscience is remarkably untroubled," Halliday responded. "Are you thinking that I am in some way responsible for your unfortunate mishap this afternoon?"

"Naturally not." Here Fitzroy allowed himself a little bitterness. "I hold Jocko personally responsible for that. It was *you*, however, not Jocko, that appropriated my quizzing glass, Hal."

"And if you *must* have another, Fitzroy, we will—as I told you—go to Rundell and Bridge and order it. I have told you more than once, though, that you would be much better off without it. You require no such affectation."

Having drawn the response he wished and created the necessary diversion, Fitzroy prepared to move in with his real question.

"Perhaps you should dance this evening, Hal, since the company in the card room will not be to your taste. Surely you will be able to find at least one lady worthy of your attention."

"All things are possible, Fitzroy . . . or so you have told me."

Halliday's brief answer and subsequent silence indicated that he would not enlarge upon this interesting subject. Fitzroy, dissatisfied, tried once again.

"You do at least know Miss Leigh," he pointed out. "You could stand up with her."

"I could," Halliday acknowledged. "I *could*, of course, dance with any of a number of ladies."

Fitzroy knew this to be perfectly true because, wild though he was widely considered to be, Halliday was still considered a matrimonial prize. Any number of young ladies would, doubtless, be thrown at his head by their anxious mamas—which was, of course, one reason he generally avoided this type of gathering. And never, upon any occasion, could he be tempted to cross the threshold of Almack's, that sacred temple devoted to débutantes and presided over by the high priestesses of society.

Growing impatient with his friend's responses to his questions, Fitzroy threw caution to the winds. "Dash it all, Hal! You changed your mind about coming tonight after meeting Miss Leigh this afternoon and learning that she was going to be here! Is she not the reason that you have come?"

"Let us say, Fitz, that Miss Leigh reminded me that not every young woman must be caper-witted. Until today, I had thought it a requirement of the youthful portion of that sex."

To his horror, Fitzroy saw that Hal's observation, although undoubtedly sincere, had not been well received by those about them. The young woman on the stairs ahead of them turned to stare at both gentlemen. Her mother also turned, fixing her fish-cold eyes on Halliday. Unperturbed, he made them a gentlemanly bow.

"Really, Hal, you see that you *must* remember

your company!" scolded Fitzroy in a low voice, anguished by such a lapse of manners.

For a moment he doubted the wisdom of bringing his friend into such a situation. The evening might well offer more social pitfalls than he had anticipated. Halliday, he knew, had not attended such an event as this in several years, declaring that he despised such insipid pastimes, and had instead devoted himself to gaming and sports and occasionally to questionable female companionship—questionable because the ladies were either married or quite ineligible.

Fitzroy had feared that Halliday was on an inevitable road to ruin, but the near loss of his fortune a year ago had sobered him somewhat. Though still heedless and wild to a fault, he no longer appeared bent on self-destruction. To Fitzroy's great relief, he had recently even given up the opera-dancer that he had been seeing for months, noting that her company had grown tiresome. All in all, Fitzroy felt that there was now reason to hope that Halliday could be brought back into the fold of proper society.

With this end in mind, he sought out Miss Leigh as soon as they had greeted their hostess and managed to gain entrance to the ballroom. To his satisfaction, he saw that she was dancing and that her movements were graceful. Her gown, although of finer materials than her walking dress of the afternoon, was nonetheless dark, with only a knot of scarlet ribbons at the bosom. The simplicity of the design suited her, and the darkness of her gown and her hair set off her fair complexion to perfection. A glance at Halliday revealed that he also had seen the young lady and was watching her.

When the music stopped, Fitzroy began to thread his way toward Miss Leigh, but Halliday was well ahead of him and was very soon leading her onto the floor. Fitzroy, shocked but pleased, hurried to claim another partner.

"You dance well, Miss Leigh," Halliday complimented her. It was unusual for him to be so nearly at eye level with his partner, but he found it very pleasant.

"Thank you, Mr. Halliday. It must be surprising to happen upon a dancing may-pole," she said, but her smile and the lightness of her tone removed any edge from her comment.

"I cannot say that I would ever have thought of you in those terms, ma'am," he returned, "but I assure you that I have a great fondness for may-poles."

Violet laughed, pleased with his light response. She had not been certain what she thought of this man after their exchange this afternoon, although she was disposed to like him for his kind remarks about her father.

"That is greatly to your credit, sir. It is, I fear, not everyone's reaction. I have found that it can be disconcerting to be staring over your partner's head while dancing, and it seems to be often equally disconcerting to the gentleman."

"Then we are fortunate in being well matched, Miss Leigh."

His dark eyes were bright as he moved past her in the figure of the dance, and she was grateful that she had a few moments away from him to be certain of her composure. She was not yet accustomed to being the subject of even so slight a gallantry. Having lived her life in the shadow of her mother, she did not expect compliments, and those that she had received since the beginning of her season had not touched her, made as they often were with grace but little sincerity. She had watched men paying court to her mother for too many years not to recognize false coin when she saw it. She was, however, most unaccountably drawn to Travis Halliday, even though she recognized in him the signs of a practiced flirt.

Fitzroy joined them at the close of the set, eager to claim Miss Leigh's hand for the next dance and to see for himself how matters had gone. To his astonishment, Halliday informed him that Miss Leigh was to be his partner for the next dance as well, but that Fitzroy could join them at supper, should he so desire. Stunned by the success of his scheme, he watched Halliday lead her out once more and retired to a corner to consider what he could do to encourage this unexpectedly promising development.

"The absence of Jocko must make the evening seem sadly flat," observed Halliday, watching his partner's face and enjoying the sudden light that sprang to her eyes at his comment.

"You are correct, of course," Violet responded demurely. "However, I feared that Mr. Fitzroy might be reluctant to meet Jocko so soon after their first encounter."

For a moment Halliday allowed himself the amusing vision of a meeting between Fitz and his nemesis on the ballroom floor. "Very wise," he agreed, nodding. "Fitzroy might well find such a meeting overwhelming, but Jocko's presence would undoubtedly enliven the evening."

"There can be no doubt of that," said Violet. "He has certainly already enlivened our life at home. Mama came upon him in her dressing room, scattering powder and wearing her favorite India shawl."

"Is she still pleased that she requested the monkey?" he asked, envisioning the scene she had described.

"Oh yes. Mama is seldom overset by such minor matters. She put the shawl away and a maid cleaned up the mess while Jocko and Mama went downstairs, hand-in-hand. She is greatly taken with Jocko's quizzing glass, which I believe he will wear from now until his death."

"Your mother must be a very patient woman. I believe not many would have had such a reaction."

Violet smiled. "Mama is seldom troubled by anything other than unhappiness. She cannot bear to see her children unhappy, or to be unhappy herself."

"And so you are always happy, Miss Leigh?" he inquired, eyebrows raised.

She met his eyes with composure. "There is very little point in being otherwise, Mr. Halliday. If I cannot alter a situation, I can at least choose how I will react to it. Why should I choose to be miserable when it will do me no good and will dash the high spirits of those I love?"

He smiled into her eyes once more and raised her hand to his lips as they moved toward one another in the dance. "You are too good to be true, Miss Leigh," he whispered. "I fear I shall awaken in the morning and find that you are a creature of my dreams."

Violet felt her cheeks grow warm, but she carefully kept her manner light. "Ah, sir," she replied, looking concerned. "Are you given to dreams of may-poles?"

"Only to particularly elegant ones, all darkness and cream and festooned with scarlet ribbons," he said, his eyes never leaving hers.

Violet no longer wondered about her mother's enjoyment of such compliments. It was most agreeable, she found—or at least it was when the gentleman was both handsome and sincere. A pleasing warmth coursed through her veins and it seemed to her that her slippers scarcely touched the polished floor. Travis Halliday seemed an intoxicating blend of stranger and friend, of the tantalizing unknown and the comfortable known, and she was suddenly deeply grateful to Jocko for his escapade.

Since a lady was permitted only two dances with a gentleman, Halliday left Mrs. Emerson's ball after sharing supper with Violet and Fitzroy, but not before receiving permission to call upon Violet the next day. Although Fitzroy would have preferred not to leave so early, he had no intention of allowing Halliday to wander off to spend the rest of the evening in objectionable company, possibly even in one of the low taverns in the East End. Instead, he firmly escorted his friend back to White's to while away the remainder of the evening and to keep his thoughts, when possible, fixed upon Miss Leigh, whom Fitzroy now saw as a beacon of hope.

"And, so, what did you think of Miss Leigh?" he inquired casually, as they settled themselves by a comfortable fire to ward off the chill of the April evening.

Knowing full well that Fitzroy was dying to know everything he was thinking upon that topic, Halliday shrugged, equally casual in his manner.

"She is charmingly unspoiled," he responded briefly, keeping his eyes fixed on the flickering fire.

Disappointed, Fitzroy tried again. "Charming in the fashion of her mother, do you think?" he inquired, for Mrs. Leigh was quite well known among the members of the *ton*. "It is always said that Mrs. Leigh's charm matches her beauty."

Halliday shook his head. "I said that Miss Leigh is unspoiled, Fitz," he pointed out, "whereas her mother knows her own worth very well. Both ladies seem to have amiable natures—but for very different reasons, I believe."

Fitzroy sat up a little straighter at this hopeful tidbit. "What is the difference, do you think?"

"Mrs. Leigh is amiable because it would be too great a trouble to be otherwise. Her daughter is so because she has chosen to be so."

Fitzroy leaned back in his chair and allowed himself to close his eyes for a moment. He was very fond of Halliday, and his friend's self-destructive behavior had troubled Fitzroy. Now he believed he could see Halliday setting his feet on solid ground once more. A wife like Miss Leigh could provide him with the stability he so sorely needed.

Any indication on his part would, he knew, be enough to drive Halliday in the opposite direction, so Fitzroy chose his words carefully.

"She does seem an agreeable young woman," he murmured, keeping his eyes closed as though he were not intent upon the conversation. Halliday's response, however, caused him to open his eyes abruptly and sit bolt-upright in his chair.

"She is indeed," answered Halliday. "If she is truly

the woman I believe her to be, Fitz, I shall marry her."

If he had said that he planned to move to the West Indies the next morning and never return, Fitzroy could not have been more astounded. Before he could recover his powers of speech, he looked at his friend searchingly to see if Halliday was simply trying to bamboozle him, but he could see no sign of it.

"It was plain that you enjoyed her company, Hal," he managed to say at last, "but I confess I had no notion that you had gone top over tail over her."

"I haven't—and that is one reason that we shall deal together very well. However, she is, as I said, a most agreeable, pleasant girl . . . and a sensible one, who has learned how to make the best of her life no matter the circumstances. She is not a woman who will natter away at a man about meaningless things, clinging to his sleeve all the while. Nor will she create an uncomfortable atmosphere in my home. On the contrary, with Miss Leigh at Bellington, my household will run smoothly and pleasantly. I shall be delighted with my visits there."

Fitzroy scrutinized him for a moment, considering the possible reasons for this marriage, and it did not take him long to arrive at the answer.

"So you have sold off all the property that is not entailed and run through all your ready, Hal. And now you need your grandfather's inheritance." He did not ask; instead, he stated these as observations.

Halliday looked at him, smiling slightly. "How well you know me and my circumstances, Hal. I do indeed need that inheritance. I am, I fear, badly dipped. It would have been much more considerate of my grandfather not to attach such a stipulation to his money."

Halliday had inherited Bellington and its attendant properties, as well as a substantial fortune, upon his father's death some five years earlier. The fortune left by his grandfather to his only grandchild had been left with stipulations. Halliday would have access to it upon his thirty-fifth birthday, which was six years distant, or upon his marriage to an eligible young woman. Approval of the young woman was to be given by Halliday's parents or, in the event of their deaths, by his grandfather's solicitor.

"Very farsighted of him, I think. Had he not done so, you would have already run through that money as well. I thought you were doing better, Hal—that you were not risking so much in your gambling." Fitzroy could not keep the disappointment from his voice.

Halliday rose and walked to the fire, standing with his back to his friend. "And so I was, Fitz. Almost losing everything last year brought me up short and caused me to assess my situation."

"Then what has happened? You won the money back from Rosing the next night, as well as the property that you had wagered."

Halliday nodded, still staring into the fire. "So I did, and I believed that I had emerged unscathed from my madness. I discovered last week, however, that I would have truly been in the suds if I had *not* managed to win the property back from Rosing, because it was not mine to lose."

Fitzroy stared at him. "What do you mean, Hal? How could it not be yours?"

"What I discovered was something that not even my father's man of business was privy to. My father had mortgaged several parcels of land in order to restore part of Bellington—and, apparently, to cover some of his own debts of honor."

"How did you find this out, Hal?" Fitzroy feared that he knew precisely how his friend had come to this knowledge.

"As you might expect, Fitz." Halliday smiled and kept his voice light. "I received a visit from the moneylender who had granted my father a very generous five years to pay off his debt. Since I most certainly could not pay it and since the moneylender holds the deeds of sale, the land will very soon be his."

"And so you must marry—and marry quickly," mused Fitzroy. "And therefore the consuming interest in Miss Leigh."

Halliday nodded. "Meeting her was indeed a stroke of good luck, Fitz. I had feared that I would be forced to make a marriage of convenience that would yoke me with a female whose company I could not endure. Such is not the case with Miss Leigh. With her as wife, I will be able to continue my present style of life, and when I go to Bellington or when she chooses to visit London, our meetings will be comfortable. She is a godsend."

Fitzroy cleared his throat. "I agree that she would be a prize for you, Hal, even without a fortune of her own or great beauty, but have you considered that Miss Leigh might not wish to marry you?"

Halliday laughed. "You are amusing, Fitz. What woman does not wish to be mistress of her own household and have her own pin money instead of becoming a general dogsbody for her family? I am not so great a coxcomb as to say Miss Leigh will fall in love with me, but I believe she is a sensible woman who will recognize such a marriage as an advantage to her."

"Well, I admit that you might have an advantage over a household with two harum-scarum youngsters and Jocko to care for," Fitzroy conceded.

"You humble me, Fitz." Halliday's dark eyes danced, and he began to look more like his normal devil-may-care self as he anticipated a comfortable future with the pressing problems of the moment all behind him. "I had not thought of the matter as a choice between Jocko and me, but I see that you are quite correct—and that the advent of Jocko has given me a great advantage."

"I hope so," said Fitzroy, grimly remembering the fate of his glass. "However, you might consider the possibility that they will all come to live with you at Bellington."

CHAPTER 4

The first weeks of Violet's season had been mildly enjoyable, but not particularly exciting. As the daughter of an accredited beauty and a well-liked gentleman, she had been received kindly enough and had naturally been the recipient of a voucher to the hallowed precincts of Almack's. She never lacked for partners at balls and she had been the object of the casual attentions of a few young fribbles who enjoyed her humor and her sense of style.

She had, however, received no offers as yet, although she had the uneasy notion that one or two of her cavaliers were toying with the notion, not because of any romantic attachment but because she was from a respectable family and would bring to her marriage an equally respectable portion. Upon her death the previous spring Great-Aunt Agatha had left her small fortune to Violet, so Violet's prospects of marriage had increased quite substantially. Nonetheless, all that she wished to do was to finish her season and return home to Richland, having done her duty to her mother, who had been looking forward to this event for years.

The night of Daisy Emerson's ball, however, Violet went home with a very different attitude toward her remaining weeks in London. She had been distinguished by the attentions of an extraordinarily appealing gentleman, and the experience had brought the additional satisfaction of discovering that she had been the envy of countless other women. She was not, she hoped, small-minded, and she had never been given to jealousy, but the unfamiliar sensation of power that washed over her when she saw Delight Ashton's expression as she was dancing with Mr. Halliday had been heady stuff indeed.

"What a triumph for you, my dear!" her mother crowed in their carriage. "To think that Travis Halliday sought you out, Violet, and danced with *no* one but you! His attentions could not have been more pointed! That is quite enough, my dear, to secure your place in the *ton*. The other girls will be *wild* with envy!"

She inspected her daughter's face as they passed a pair of linkboys with their torches. "Did you find him charming, Violet?" She patted Violet's hand encouragingly, inviting confidences.

Violet schooled her expression carefully. She did not wish to admit to any decided partiality, nor did she wish to bring herself more intensely under inspection than she already was.

She smiled back at her mother. "Yes, of course, Mama. How could one not find him so?"

"Naturally no one could resist him, Violet. You are quite in the right of it. And you did very well, dear. No one could see anything save the fact that you were having a pleasant time."

"And so I was," Violet agreed, shivering slightly as she remembered his touch.

"Are you cold, dearest?" asked Mrs. Leigh, immediately catching up an extra shawl from the seat of the carriage to wrap about Violet's shoulders. "April evenings can chill to the bone and we cannot have you take ill, Violet—not just now, when Mr. Halliday will be coming to call."

At the thought of seeing him again, Violet fell victim to another fit of shivering, and her mother was occupied during the rest of the ride with keeping her warm and informing her that she would have a cup of chamomile tea before going to sleep in a bed warmed by a hot brick.

Once she was safely tucked into a warm bed, Violet indulged herself in the enjoyment of reliving the evening. It had all been delightful, but before drifting off to sleep, she reminded herself firmly that, regardless of his request to call upon her, she should have no expectation of any such thing occurring. By the time morning arrived, sanity would prevail, and he would recall that she was indeed what Delight Ashton had once called her—an animated may-pole—and she would see him no more.

Nonetheless, she dressed very carefully the next morning, spending more time than usual in choosing her dress and preparing her hair. Her mother assisted by awakening at what was for her an unusually early hour and drifting in and out of Violet's room, cup of chocolate in hand, to comment upon her daughter's choices.

"Oh, I *do* think you should wear the golden merino with crimson ruching that I had made for you, love—so *very* smart, you must admit," she said, eyeing with distaste the plain gown that her daughter had chosen.

"It is indeed excessively smart, Mama, but it looks

very much like you and not at all like me. I should look as though I were attiring myself to be in a show at Astley's Amphitheater if I were to wear it."

She tempered her words with a smile to keep her mother from being hurt, but it was a constant trial to avoid wearing the gowns her mother chose for her. Instead of the merino, she wore a severely plain morning gown in the same shade of violet as her eyes and added only a paisley shawl to ward off the chill.

"You look charming, Violet," Mrs. Leigh conceded, and together they went downstairs to await their callers.

They were not long in coming. Mrs. Leigh always had a gathering of admirers, particularly after a ball, and she reveled in their attentions. This morning there were two or three older gentlemen, all bearing nosegays.

Violet, too, had a scattering of attendants, the young men who had chosen her as their particular lady for the season, gathering in her drawing room to pay her compliments that they had labored over and refined and to idle away part of another indolent day.

They did not trouble her, and Adrian had taken to referring to them as "Vi's lapdogs." She knew that their attentions were as frivolous as their natures, and she paid scant attention to them, assuming that they had nowhere else to spend their mornings. One unfortunate young man, James Wyatt, had taken to writing poetry, a calling for which he clearly had no talent. This morning he had an ode written in praise of Violet's eyebrows, which he stammeringly read to the accompaniment of hoots from his friends.

In the midst of this, a large bouquet of hothouse roses arrived for Violet, and the card informed her that Mr. Halliday would always remember last night's ball—and yesterday's interlude with Jocko—and that he longed to see her again. Mrs. Leigh had them arranged in a place of honor in the drawing room and overset Violet by giving her deeply meaningful glances, looking from her daughter to the flowers and back once more.

At last Mr. Halliday appeared in the entrance of the drawing room, and Violet discovered that it was possible for a heart to leap. She felt the pulse at the base of her neck throbbing, but she did her best to smile at him coolly as he bowed over her hand.

"You look very fresh this morning, Miss Leigh," he said, his eyes approving. "No one would suspect that you had danced the night away."

Scarcely a lover-like beginning, Violet thought to herself, but then, she had told herself to have no expectations. She smiled up at him. "Then you, sir, having danced only two sets, must be feeling very fresh indeed."

Overlooking the significant throat-clearing of the young poet, who was hoping to capture Violet's attention once more, Mr. Halliday escorted her to a window overlooking the street and indicated a handsome curricle waiting below, its spirited blacks being held in check by a diminutive tiger.

"I had hoped, Miss Leigh, that you might look sadly worn by last night's ball, so that I could offer you a ride in Rotten Row to restore you—but you have quite undone me by looking as bright as a button."

Violet appeared to think the matter over. "I do, as

a matter of fact, feel slightly out of frame," she said slowly. "And, with so many engagements today, this might well be my only opportunity for a breath of fresh air. Perhaps in a few minutes, when my callers have left—"

It was at that moment that Jocko made his entrance upon the scene. He had been carefully restricted to Adrian's chamber and had managed only one major escape thus far, when he had made free with Mrs. Leigh's dressing room. It was clear, however, that he had once more managed an escape. This time an unwary maid had not been quick enough in closing the door, and Jocko had triumphantly fled to the stairway. Hearing the sound of voices, he had hastened down the steps to add his mite to the conviviality.

Jocko paused in the entrance of the drawing room for a moment, then, recognizing a friend in Mr. Halliday, hurried over to renew the acquaintance. He sprang to that gentleman's arms in one quick movement, chittering and patting Halliday's cheek approvingly as he raised the glass to his eye so that he could be certain his friend was enjoying good health. The other gentlemen in the drawing room broke into laughter, while Mrs. Leigh rang for her butler.

Adrian came pounding down the stairs, with Cynthia hard on his heels. Jocko, seeing them enter with the butler, recognized that his freedom was about to be curtailed and, with a plaintive cry, made for higher ground. The drapes were his first port of call, but they did not support his anxious scrabbling well and descended to the carpet in a gentle cascade of golden brocade, whereupon he sprang to the top of the pianoforte and from there to another drapery.

The young gentlemen entered into the spirit of the fray and began to enact a battle plan to herd Jocko into a corner of the room, where they would capture him by tossing Mr. Wyatt's coat over him. Mr. Wyatt seemed disposed to protest this abuse of his wardrobe, but he was overridden and the jacket wrested from him. Cynthia, in the meanwhile, punctuated the furor with shrill appeals to Jocko and to Adrian, while the little maid who had allowed the escape sobbed into her apron in the passage.

"It seems to me, Miss Leigh, that this would be the very moment to make our exit," he murmured, just as the gentlemen began to close in on the chattering Jocko, who responded by pelting them with roses snatched from Violet's bouquet.

Violet required no encouragement, and together they hurried from the scene of chaos, not pausing to look back. She felt strangely exhilarated. Instead of remaining inside to help to restore order and calm, as she would normally have done, she had abandoned them all and thought only of what she wished to do. She felt extraordinarily free, even though she was only going for a curricle ride.

The day was soft and pleasant, the company charming, and Violet's view from the curricle without compare. If she was a little chilly, not having paused to change into appropriate clothing, she did not truly feel it. Talking with her companion occupied her thoughts and the freshness of the spring day lifted her spirits until she felt as though she had been drinking champagne. As they drove among the fashionable throng, she noticed with pleasure the same envious glances that she had received last night. Until the past day, she could not have imagined how satisfying it was to know that others wished themselves in her place.

At last, however, she reluctantly brought their impromptu outing to a close, remembering that she and her mother had an engagement with friends later that day and not wishing to cause her mother to miss it.

"Shall I see you tonight, Miss Leigh?" he inquired, turning to look at her.

"How can I say, sir?" she responded, smiling. "I shall be at Covent Garden, but I do not know where you will be."

"Surely you know better than that, ma'am," he said reprovingly. "You may be certain that I, too, shall be at Covent Garden."

Violet smiled to herself. So this was what it was like to be admired, she thought. It was nothing at all like the mindless compliments bestowed upon her by the callow young men she had met thus far—young men lacking in humor and style. How extraordinary it seemed that such a gentleman as Travis Halliday had selected her.

Adrian, having seen them leave in the curricle, had been watching for their return, determined to have a closer look at that handsome equipage and the fine bits of blood and bone that were pulling it. When Halliday arrived in front of the house and the tiger sprang down, Adrian hurried out to accost them and Violet went inside, abandoning her escort to his fate. If he could hold his own with Jocko, she reasoned, Adrian could present no great challenge.

Inside, the house had been restored to its former order and to reasonable quiet. In short, there was no sign of Jocko.

Violet entered cautiously and hurried to her room to change. She was prepared when her mother was ready to leave, but she had scarcely managed it, for Adrian had come upstairs and insisted upon giving her a detailed account of the glories of the curricle and its cattle, which he was certain she had not fully appreciated.

"I told Halliday I'd tried to convince Mama to get me a curricle like his, but that she'd told me I'd have to wait," he added disconsolately. Then he brightened, recovering his usual cheerful nature. "And he laughed when I told him I'd tried to get 'round Mama by persuading you to give me the ready after Great-Aunt Agatha cocked up her toes. He's a great gun!"

"Honestly, Adrian, how can you be so rag-mannered?" she demanded, shocked by his indelicate reference to their great-aunt's death as well as by his discussing money with someone who was scarcely more than a stranger.

"He likes you, Vi," Adrian concluded with a wink, unshaken by her reprimand. "We were talking about Jocko and he said you and Mama must have the patience of saints . . . and he said he was looking forward to seeing how Jocko liked traveling in a carriage when we go back to Richland. Sounds as though he intends to be around to see it."

Knowing full well that she would not be able to bring Adrian to a sense of his poor conduct, Violet allowed herself to be fobbed off with her brother's final comment. The thought that Mr. Halliday planned to be a part of her future was more than acceptable.

Their call on Lady Dismore, an elderly woman who had been a friend of her grandmother, began in a manner fully as dull as Violet had anticipated it would be. She was untroubled, however, both because such things seldom ruffled her and because she had the evening to anticipate. She knew that she would see Mr. Halliday again and that he would manage to take her apart from the others for at least a few minutes of private conversation. Already she found herself looking forward to time spent in his company, and yet she had known him only a day. Violet marveled at the fact that a single day should make such a difference in her life—and that a man who had been a stranger yesterday now seemed so much a friend.

She was called sharply back to the present when she found herself addressed by Mrs. Digby, one of Lady Dismore's companions and friends. Mrs. Leigh had been regaling the ladies with an account of Jocko's first excursion in London, and her story had caught their attention. Mr. Halliday, it appeared, was the grandson of a man who had been a friend of Lady Dismore.

"And so you have met Travis Halliday," Mrs. Digby said, her small, bright eyes fixed on Violet's face.

"Indeed I have had that pleasure," Violet agreed. "Is he a friend of yours as well, Mrs. Digby?"

Mrs. Digby tittered. "Of mine? I should think not! I am scarcely in the habit of frequenting gambling hells!"

"Come now, Mrs. Digby," Mrs. Leigh said lightly. "He is a most charming man. You are too hard upon poor Mr. Halliday."

"Nonsense!" Here Mrs. Digby turned to Lady Dismore for support. "You know as well as I do, Lydia, that his behavior is scandalous! Why, he all but ruined himself just last year!"

Lady Dismore nodded sadly. "Quite shocking it was, to think that Howard's grandson would do such a thing."

"Ruined himself? What do you mean?" asked Violet, puzzled.

"Gambled away everything in his estate that wasn't nailed down," replied Mrs. Digby, clearly enjoying every moment of the conversation. "But then he sat down with the same man the next night and won everything back. Now, if that doesn't make him a hardened gamester, I don't know what would!"

"That is scarcely a rarity, however," said Mrs. Leigh, coming once more to his defense. She had seen that Violet enjoyed that gentleman's company, and she had no wish to have it all come to naught because of Mrs. Digby's penchant for gossip. "I daresay most of the gentlemen of the *ton* have done their share of gambling. It is not to be wondered at that a young man should follow their lead."

"And *I* wonder that you stand up for him, Mrs. Leigh," sniffed Mrs. Digby. Lady Dismore was, she knew, very fond of Marianne Leigh, but Mrs. Digby had always considered her too careless in her conduct. "I should think that you would wish to protect your daughter from a man such as that! Certainly that was *my* only interest in bringing up such a matter!"

Mrs. Leigh looked at Mrs. Digby as though she doubted that, and Violet certainly mistrusted the lady's motives. Mrs. Digby's eyes were bright and eager, searching for anything she might be able to glean. She might consider Mr. Halliday a hardened gamester, but she herself was just as clearly a hardened gossip.

"Indeed?" responded Mrs. Leigh coolly.

"Yes, of course," Mrs. Digby assured her, but before she could continue, Lady Dismore spoke, her mind still on the past.

"He was wild, even as a boy," she said sadly. "Just like his father before him. I had thought Howard too hard on Travis when he made out his will, but it seems he was quite in the right of it. If he had not kept the money from him until he was thirty-five, I daresay it might already all be gone."

"Thirty-five?" gasped Mrs. Leigh. "That seems an excessively long time to be forced to wait for one's inheritance!"

Lady Dismore tapped her cane absently and shook her head. "You see what he would have done," she said. "He would have made ducks and drakes of it, just as he has with everything that was available to him."

"Still," insisted Mrs. Leigh, "it seems most unwise to make him wait so long! That in itself might be enough to encourage the kind of behavior you describe."

Lady Dismore shook her head. "Howard provided that the boy could have the money earlier if he married a steady sort of young woman that Howard approved. If Travis wishes to settle down and have access to the money, he has only to make a good marriage."

Violet saw her mother flash her a lightning-quick glance. "I see," she murmured.

Seizing the moment to add her own *on-dit*, Mrs. Digby lowered her voice and leaned toward the others, as though they might be overheard by passersby on the street. "And naturally he will do no such thing! He has no intention of giving up his scandalous ways! It is not just his gambling, after all! Why, his love affairs are notorious!" She leaned closer still, and added, "You know all about Anna Aubrey, do you not?"

Mrs. Leigh and Violet exchanged an apprehensive glance.

"Who is Anna Aubrey?" asked Mrs. Leigh in a voice suitably low.

Mrs. Digby lowered her voice still more. "Mr. Halliday's opera-dancer, of course—or at least his most recent one," she replied. "I understand that he has kept her for more than a year now."

Violet could see that her mother carefully avoided her eye as she responded.

"But that is true of many gentlemen, Mrs. Digby, as you must know. And are you quite certain of your information?" she replied.

The lady tittered again, pleased to be able to confirm her comments. "Of course I am, Mrs. Leigh. You have only to ask Lydia. She has seen them together, too."

A glance in Lady Dismore's direction was all that was needed. She nodded, and Violet acknowledged to herself what she had suspected all along.

Travis Halliday was not for her.

CHAPTER 5

Going to the theater that night required all of Violet's determination. She knew that she would see Mr. Halliday there, and she had promised herself that she would allow no knowledge of his recently discovered interests to escape her. She knew that, for her own peace of mind, she would have to put a period to their relationship, but she wished to retain her dignity while doing so. Hearing about the importance to him of a suitable wife had fully explained to her why he had shown such a marked and unexpected interest in such an unlikely lady.

Little did Lady Dismore and Mrs. Digby realize that Mr. Halliday had finally decided to take the painful step necessary to claiming his inheritance, she thought with dry amusement. He would, however, be obliged to find some other steady young woman to be his bride. Violet had considerable self-respect, and she had not the slightest intention of allowing herself to enter a marriage that promised nothing but heartache.

She was, she knew, already too fond of Travis Halliday, and she had allowed herself to be duped into thinking that he was equally taken with her. Now that she was aware his motivations, as well as his history of his gambling and love affairs, she could no more subject herself to such certain unhappiness than she could leap from a high cliff into the sea. She would go home to Richland and to the quiet, sure existence that had been predicted for her by Great-Aunt Matilda. That at least guaranteed peace of mind. She and Jocko could grow old together, she thought with grim amusement.

Her mother had done her best to undo the damage done by Mrs. Digby, but she had made no progress. Violet had recognized Halliday as a flirt, and she knew that she was scarcely the type of woman to attract such a man, but she had allowed herself to be taken in by his charm. Now she knew just why he had sought her out again after their first encounter. She had no doubt that she was to be the acceptable young woman—dull to a fault—that would allow him to claim his inheritance. She said nothing of any of this to her mother, but Mrs. Leigh realized that her daughter was paying little attention to her attempts to excuse Travis Halliday.

Violet dressed carefully for the evening, replying absently to Adrian and Cynthia when they came to her door with Jocko, who was intent upon providing her with a little entertainment before she left for the theater. She felt as though she were viewing everything from behind a sheet of glass. No real contact could be made—even with Jocko.

"How splendid you look, my dear!" exclaimed Mrs. Leigh, determined to raise her daughter's spirits. She could cheerfully have throttled Mrs. Digby for providing so much unwanted information. The becoming animation of the morning had left Violet's face and she looked pale and withdrawn, though elegantly gowned and shod.

Violet made an effort to smile, knowing how her mother would fret if she felt she was unhappy. "And you look as you always do, Mama: delightful enough to turn every head in a room."

Her observation was no more than the truth, and it had the inevitable happy effect of turning Mrs. Leigh's thoughts to more pleasant subjects.

"I thought of wearing the gown of cherry-red silk," Mrs. Leigh replied, "but then I decided to choose something a little more delicate."

"And your choice was divine, Mama, as always." Violet spoke with sincerity, for in her gown of celestial blue crepe, a shawl of silver net floating about her shoulders, Mrs. Leigh did look angelic.

Satisfied with her appearance and diverted for the moment from thoughts of her daughter's unhappiness, Mrs. Leigh tripped down the front steps to the waiting carriage. Violet followed quietly in her wake, eager to have the evening over with. In fact, she was now anxious to have all of the trials and tribulations of the season behind her so that she could retreat once more to the peace and safety of Richland. Her mother would be disappointed, of course, but it would not be long before Cynthia would have her coming-out, and Mrs. Leigh would then enjoy a season with a daughter who was sought after by every eligible gentleman of the *ton.*

Not even the enjoyable bustle of Covent Garden, with its amusing spectacle of young bloods on the strut and ladies on parade, dowagers in turbans and courtesans in rouge and powder, could divert her as it usually would. They were sharing a box with friends of Mrs. Leigh, and fortunately Violet was not called upon to do more than murmur a few pleasantries upon their arrival and to smile blandly at the conversation of the others. They were the guests of Mrs. Pearson, a tiny woman in a white sarsenet gown and a purple turban, topped with an ostrich feather calculated to add a foot to her diminutive height. She was accompanied by two other ladies and two very attentive gentlemen. Violet was relieved to blend into the background, watching the play absently and trying to avoid studying the audience, searching for Mr. Halliday's now familiar profile.

She managed so well that she did, for the moment at least, forget her difficulties and become absorbed in the play unfolding below her, so it was a shock when she heard a low voice at her ear and became acutely aware of another presence in the box.

"Surely you are not watching the play, Miss Leigh?" Halliday's voice was low and teasing, his breath warm on her neck. "You do realize that the only reason for coming to the theater is to be seen and to flirt?"

She smiled stiffly. "I should imagine you do that very well, sir," she responded. "I fear that I am not so practiced as you."

"You are right," he said penitently. "I am older and I have misspent my time—but you see," he continued, taking her chin in his hand and gently turning her face toward him, "I have the best of all excuses."

"Do you indeed?" Violet asked, reminding herself sharply of the things she now knew about this man. Otherwise, she would soon find herself believing his every word. His air of sincerity was most deceptive. "And just what is the excuse, sir? I am most anxious to hear it."

He smiled at her, his dark eyes looking deeply into hers as though to affirm the deep connection between them. "Because I did not meet *you* until yesterday, Miss Leigh." His voice was tender and he lifted her hand to his lips as he spoke.

Violet was torn between believing him—despite what she knew—and snatching her hand away and rapping him smartly with her fan. She could do neither, she told herself calmly. She must remain in charge of her emotions.

"Very pretty, Mr. Halliday," she conceded, her tone distinctly condescending. "I daresay you do it so well because you have practiced your lines upon so many occasions."

He looked at her for a moment, puzzled, then laughed reluctantly as she reclaimed her hand.

"You are very hard on me, ma'am," he observed, watching her closely.

She shrugged lightly. "I have observed many flirts over the years, you see," she explained. "My mother has always attracted a train of admirers. My father used to laugh at them and the ways in which they tried to attract her attention and win her favor. So even though the experience is not my own, I have learned a very great deal through watching."

"I shall have to be very careful," he replied gravely. "I should not wish to be laughed at, as you describe."

"No," she agreed. "I am certain that must be an unpleasant experience—and one completely foreign to you, Mr. Halliday."

He stood up and held out his hand. "Do come with me for a stroll through the lobby, Miss Leigh. It will not be so crowded now as it will be at the interval, and I daresay that you might enjoy a little air."

She took his hand and rose, telling herself that going with him was a necessary step in ending the relationship, but her heart grew perceptibly lighter as he smiled at her.

They were not, she saw immediately, the only ones to decide upon a stroll. When they were first in London, she had been surprised to see that most people did not go to the theater to watch the play. They went, as Mr. Halliday had just indicated, to gossip and flirt and to be seen—and the play quite often interfered with their activities.

"You seem very distant tonight, Miss Leigh," Mr. Halliday observed. "Is anything amiss?"

She forced a light smile and a still lighter tone. "Oh no, sir. How should there be anything wrong?"

"I thought perhaps Jocko had set upon you before you could leave this evening," he returned, still watching her closely. "Or perhaps your brother or sister has a problem that required your attention."

"No, neither my family nor Jocko has caused me the slightest problem—at least, not after Jocko had the adventure you witnessed this morning." Violet was pleased that she could speak with truth upon this point.

"Then has something else occurred to overset you?" he asked.

Violet frowned a little and looked at him directly. "Why do you think that something is troubling me, Mr. Halliday?"

He stopped and turned to meet her eyes. "Because you have lost your usual playfulness, Miss Leigh. If there is something I might do to restore it, I should wish to do so."

There was a pause, and then he added, "You are quite delightful to talk with, you know . . . but tonight you do not appear to wish to talk at all."

Violet lowered her eyes, fearful that he was able to see far too much about her already. "I fear I have the headache," she murmured, hating herself for retreating behind such a frail excuse.

"Then let us find you a place to sit and I will find you something cool to drink," he replied, looking around for a likely place.

Only moments later she was seated in a snug little corner behind a potted plant, sipping a glass of ratafia.

"There is no need to talk, Miss Leigh. Just close your eyes if you wish, and if you think it necessary, I will be glad to escort you home."

Violet shook her head. "Pray do not trouble yourself, sir. I shall be quite all right." She took another sip. "In fact, I am already feeling much more the thing. Perhaps it would be best if I went back to our box."

She started to rise, but he caught her wrist and kept her beside him. "Are you certain that you feel well enough to go back?" he asked.

She managed an easy smile. "Of course I am. There is no need to fuss over me."

"Ah, but I wish to fuss over you, Miss Leigh. I think that perhaps you are the one that is always looking after others, and I should like to change that."

He was far too perceptive, Violet thought with distaste. Of course it was an unaccustomed pleasure to her to have someone else make her welfare his first concern. He read her far too easily.

To her dismay, he took her other hand as well and drew her closer to him. "I should like to have the right to look after you and fuss over you forever, Miss Leigh. Dare I hope that you would let me?"

Violet caught her breath. She had not expected his proposal to be so quickly or boldly made.

"You are asking me to marry you, Mr. Halliday?" she asked, giving herself a little time to collect herself.

"You know that I am, Miss Leigh. You will be mistress of my home and my heart. Tell me that you will allow me that honor and I will call upon your mother for her permission as soon as dawn breaks tomorrow."

Even in the midst of her emotional turmoil, the sudden image of anyone calling upon Mrs. Leigh at the break of dawn called forth an involuntary smile.

He saw it, but mistook its meaning. "Ah, I can see that you wish to accept my offer, ma'am. You will make me a very happy man, and I swear that I shall make you a happy woman."

Violet shook her head hastily. "No—you misunderstand me, Mr. Halliday. I appreciate the honor that you do me by asking for my hand," she said, almost choking on the insincerity of those words, "but I assure you that I have no desire to marry you."

Halliday looked as though someone had unexpectedly emptied a pitcher of cold water over his head. For a moment he only stared at her, words having left him.

"I apologize, Miss Leigh," he said quietly. "I should not have asked you when you are not feeling well. It was ill-advised on my part, and I shall wait until a better time and make my offer in a more suitable place."

Again she shook her head. "I assure you, Mr. Halliday, that there is no need to make your offer a second time. I have absolutely no intention of accepting it whether you make it tomorrow or two years hence, here at Covent Garden or in the Alps of Switzerland. I have no interest in accepting your proposal."

"I see." His lips were tight and the laughter had left his eyes. She should, she knew, feel some satisfaction in seeing that the rejection pained him, but that feeling evaded her.

All that she felt was emptiness as she rose abruptly and quickly made her way back to the box to join the others. She was vaguely aware that he was with her, escorting her, that he made his bow to her and murmured his good-bye.

Violet never had the slightest notion of what happened in the rest of the play, of what was said during the intervals, or of how she got home that evening and put herself to bed.

She received a stiff note from Travis Halliday the next morning, apologizing for trespassing upon her good nature and wishing her well. As he closed, he informed her that by the time she read the note, he would be on a ship to the West Indies, so she could be certain that she need not fear encountering him during the remainder of the season.

CHAPTER 6

"Oh really, Adrian, this is *too* wicked of you, dear boy! You promised me *faithfully* that you would not land yourself in the brambles this term, and yet here you are, sent down from Oxford once again! I really do *not* know what to do with you!"

Mrs. Leigh regarded her wayward son with all the seriousness she was able to muster, which unfortunately, thought Violet ruefully, was very little. Watching their mother attempting to scold Adrian was rather like watching a playful kitten take a greyhound to task. As always, her affectionate tone belied her words, and the object of the scolding recognized that she was weakening. He immediately fell to his knees in front of her, taking her small hands in his and lowering his head in mock penitence, although not in time to hide the merriment in his eyes.

"I humbly repent my many sins, Mama dearest. I beg you to allow me to stay here in London with you and the girls, where I will devote myself to your well-being. Pray *don't* send me away to the wilderness of Richland on a repairing lease."

Richland could scarcely be termed a wilderness, being a cultivated, pleasant estate only a half-day's journey from London, but Adrian regarded it as the back of beyond. London, with its balls and clubs and infinite variety of amusements, was much more to his taste.

Mrs. Leigh, who had much the same tastes, smiled and stroked her son's bright hair, as golden as her own. Then, catching Violet's cautioning glance, she made one last valiant attempt to reprove him.

"Your father would have been *most* distressed by your behavior, Adrian. I only wish that I knew just what *he* would have said to you under these circumstances."

He glanced up at her and grinned, abandoning even the pretense of repentance. "What absolute rubbish, Mama! You know as well as I that he was sent down himself! I daresay he would have a good laugh with me over it, and we could have compared notes on our many offenses over our port and cigars after dinner."

"I should imagine his reaction would have depended upon the reason you were sent down, Adrian." Violet did her best to sound serious, trying to harden her heart against his engaging carelessness.

She had watched the interchange between her mother and younger brother with a sinking heart. She knew, of course, that her mother would never be able to disapprove of anything that Adrian did, but she had hoped that Adrian himself might be slightly abashed by finding himself in trouble again so soon. He had not finished the previous term because he had stayed out after curfew, drinking and gambling, and now here he was, sent down once more before the end of term. He was indeed incorrigible.

"Come now, Vi, don't read me a scold and look as though you've been biting into lemons. It's nothing to fly up into the boughs over," he responded easily, rising to his feet and hugging her. "After all, everyone gets into a mill now and then."

"You've been fighting?" His mother looked at him in alarm, hurrying over to him and turning his face so that she could examine him carefully. "Are you hurt, dearest?"

"Nothing that will show," he assured her. "I landed him a facer, and that pretty well ended the fisticuffs."

"Brawling." Violet shook her head and turned away from him. "And I suppose you were in some low inn, drinking and gambling, when the fight occurred."

"Well, I was a little bit on the go," he admitted, "but not nearly so high up in the world as Jack Braun was or I could never have floored him so handily. He is a full two-stone heavier."

"Why, Adrian! You could have been badly injured!" His mother shook his arm lightly to reprove him and he patted her hand reassuringly.

"I believe that's exactly what Black Jack had in mind," he replied lightly. "But, as you see, he failed completely in his object. And, if I stay in London, I shall drop round to Gentleman Jackson's for a few more lessons. It is just as well to be able to defend oneself adequately, after all."

"Yes indeed," agreed his mother, much struck by this practical suggestion. "That is very true! By all means, Adrian, you must stay here in town. It is clearly the *prudent* thing to do."

She glanced across the room at Violet. "And we

will *all* be delighted to have you here, dearest. Won't we, Violet?"

Her daughter gave way to the inevitable with good humor. She did, after all, love her brother dearly, even if keeping him out of scrapes grew more and more impossible each year. She always missed her father, but she felt his loss more than ever when Adrian had run amuck and was in need of guidance. Their mother had the best of intentions, but she never made any real push to keep Adrian and Cynthia in order. Cynthia, just now turned sixteen, was promising to be as much a handful as Adrian.

"Of course we will," Violet replied demurely. "We are in need of someone to read to us in the evening and to squire us about to the museums during the day. I daresay we should spend tomorrow at the British Museum, don't you think so, Mama?"

It would have been difficult to say whose face fell the farthest at this glad news; both mother and brother appeared horror-struck.

"Here now, Vi! I never promised to do penance for my sins! You can't mean it!"

"Of course she doesn't," Mrs. Leigh assured him, relaxing as she remembered that she was indeed the parent and need not suffer such Turkish treatment at the hands of her daughter. "Violet is teasing! Why, after all, we have only a few days before we leave town for the holidays, and we have *countless* things to do! We must remember that Cynthia is to have her coming-out this spring, and I still have a very long list of errands to attend to."

As though on cue, Cynthia swept into the room, whirling so that Adrian could appreciate the glories of her new ball gown, a confection of white silk and gauze, spangled with stars. She ended her performance with a deep curtsey and her admiring audience applauded enthusiastically.

"You look radiant, darling!" exclaimed Mrs. Leigh, clapping her hands in delight.

"Quite celestial," agreed Adrian. "The male of the species does not stand a chance against you, Cyn. I predict that the streets will be strewn with the bodies of men that you refuse."

He strolled over to the windows and looked out at the garden in the square across the street. "We may not have enough room here, Mama," he observed. "I daresay we will need more space for those bodies."

"Goosecap!" retorted his sister, but she was smiling complacently. Her glass, she knew, did not lie to her, and she had already received enough attention to make her certain that she had only to glance toward a gentleman to enslave him.

She does indeed look radiant, thought Violet, *even celestial, given her gown.* She looked, in fact, just like their mother. Adrian, too, bore a striking resemblance, although he never acknowledged his own good looks. Violet repressed a sigh as foolish self-indulgence. *She* most certainly did not look at all like the other three, nor had she inherited their lighthearted, frivolous attitude toward life. They were like the grasshopper in the fable, and she was the dull but prudent ant.

Adrian paused suddenly in his teasing of his sister. "Do you mean to say that we're leaving for Richland in just a few days?" he asked his mother, his smile fading. It had taken some moments for her words to register fully.

"It's almost time for Christmas, Adrian," Violet reminded him. She, for one, was very grateful to be returning home. London did not hold the same appeal for her that it did for the rest of her family. "Aren't you looking forward to it?"

There was a perceptible pause and, before he could answer, Mrs. Leigh interceded, her voice bright. "Actually, children, I have a surprise for you! Not even Violet knows about it."

She glanced around the room, but the expressions of her children were cautious. Violet thought with amusement that they looked like an illustration of the old saying, "Once burnt, twice shy." They had suffered a good many of their mother's surprises over the years.

"Well?" she said finally, when no one spoke. "Isn't anyone going to ask me what it is?"

"It isn't a spa, is it?" asked Adrian anxiously. "We're not going off to drink brackish water and cat-lap in some godforsaken town inhabited by old people in nightcaps, are we?"

Mrs. Leigh, ignoring the allusion to an unsuccessful family journey to Bath, laughed gaily. "Of course not, Adrian! It is something much, much better!"

"Brighton?" asked Cynthia hopefully, thinking of all of the assemblies she could attend there so that she could practice her skills as a flirt before her London season.

Mrs. Leigh shook her head firmly. "Definitely not Brighton!"

Violet breathed a sigh of relief. For a moment she had had a terrible vision of having to chaperone the other three in the midst of the temptations of the assembly balls held at the Castle Inn and the Old Ship, the magnificence of the Tenth Hussars of Brighton Camp, along with the possible unsettling presence of the Prince Regent and his unruly crowd.

"Well, where is it to be then, Mama?" demanded Cynthia. "Where are we going?"

Mrs. Leigh glanced at Violet. "Can't *you* guess, my dear?" she asked. "The place has a special connection for you."

Violet's heart sank, and Brighton began to look much more inviting than it had. "Not Ashton Park, Mama?" she asked weakly. "Surely not Ashton Park."

Her mother's eyes lit up. "You *clever* girl! I knew that you would require only a hint."

For the length of Violet's life, her mother had insisted upon viewing a trip to Ashton Park as a particularly special treat for her daughter—and all because of Delight Ashton. Somehow, her mother had failed to note that the two girls heartily disliked one another. Since Delight's mother was a girlhood friend of Mrs. Leigh and since they had two daughters the same age, the ladies were perfectly certain that the girls were also destined to be lifelong friends. They had subjected them to the interchange of countless family visits and had even sent both the girls to the same boarding school, Miss Delaware's Seminary for Young Ladies. There had been no escape for Violet.

"Oh, Mama," she sighed. "I would *so* much prefer being at Richland for Christmas."

Although Cynthia and Adrian did not dislike Ashton Park as much as their sister, they were not overwhelmed by the notion of spending their holiday there either, and their faces revealed that clearly.

"Oh, my dears!" exclaimed Mrs. Leigh encouragingly. "It won't be *just* the Ashtons there, naturally. They are having a splendid house party, and we will have balls and charades and theatricals! It will be *delightful*!"

At this disclosure, Adrian and Cynthia began to look a little brighter.

"Do you know who else has been invited, Mama?" demanded Cynthia. "Will Lloyd Peyton be attending?"

Mrs. Leigh shook her head. "I have no idea who will be there, my dear, but I am *certain* that there will be a full company of young people, and Deirdre has informed me that every bed in the house will be taken!"

The others began to speculate about the guest list, with Cynthia punctuating the conversation with doubts as to whether she had enough gowns for the balls, and at once the atmosphere became much more cheerful. Violet, however, was not comforted. For her, the most charming assembly of guests in the world could not offset the discomfort of being a guest in Delight's home, and the thought of being a fortnight in a house that was brimful of people held little appeal for her.

Nonetheless, when her mother held out her hand to Violet to include her in the group, and when she saw how happy her mother looked, she forced herself to smile and tried to enter into the spirit of the conversation. She would have to make the best of it, she thought with resignation, just as she had done so many times before.

Little did she realize that she was, in truth, much happier at that moment than she soon would be.

The blow fell upon her like a lightning bolt the next day.

True to his word, Adrian had taken himself away in the company of two friends to visit Gentleman Jackson's, and he had informed the ladies at breakfast that they need not expect him until it was time for them to go to the theater that evening. Mrs. Leigh and Cynthia had departed soon afterwards to select ribbons and slippers and gloves for Cynthia's newest gowns and to inspect the possible addition of a swansdown muff to Cynthia's wardrobe. Violet had thought of accompanying them, but decided at the last minute to stay at home and enjoy having the drawing room to herself to read. There would be little enough time for solitude in the days to come.

She had been peacefully settled for an hour or two when she was surprised by the sounds of an arrival downstairs and then the sound of Adrian's quick, firm step on the stairs. She put down her book and looked up as he entered the room, curious as to what could have brought him home so early in the day.

He sat down next to her on the sofa and stared at her, his eyes bright. "Well, Vi dear, prepare yourself! I have news for you!"

Being told to prepare oneself for news seldom bodes well, so Violet did her best to brace herself. Her mind worked quickly, trying to think what trouble Adrian might have managed to get himself into in so short a space of time. She was still so engaged when he unleashed the lightning bolt.

"We were just going into Jackson's as a group was leaving Angelo's, which is right next door, you know."

Violet nodded. She was aware of the popularity of both establishments. Gentleman Jackson's club was for boxing, naturally, and Angelo's was a fencing academy. Gentlemen who were inclined toward sports frequented both places. Still busy with her troubled thoughts about Adrian's present difficulty, she tried to think of whom he might have encountered there.

"You didn't quarrel with anyone, did you, Adrian? Freddie and Beaver were with you, so surely you didn't quarrel." She referred to Adrian's easygoing friends, with whom he had gone out that morning. Beaver had acquired his unfortunate nickname due to his fondness for beaver hats and his rather prominent front teeth.

Her brother stared at her. "Quarrel with anyone? Why should I be quarreling with anyone, Vi?"

Relieved of the first fear that had arisen, Violet managed a smile. "Never mind, Adrian. Do tell me your news."

"Well, that's what I'm trying to do, isn't it?" he said plaintively. "Sent Freddie and Beaver along to Tattersall's without me so that I could make a special trip home to tell you."

"To tell me *what*, Adrian?" she demanded, losing patience.

He decided that directness was the best approach and plunged into the delicate matter with no further preparation. "I met Halliday coming out of Angelo's, Vi, and he stopped to have a word with me."

"Did he indeed?" she remarked without expression. Whatever she had expected, it had not been this. She had not seen Travis Halliday since the night at Covent Garden two years earlier.

She had, with some difficulty, shared the news of his proposal with her mother. To her credit, Mrs. Leigh, though disappointed, said nothing of that to Violet. Instead, for the next two days she fussed over her as though she was an invalid, keeping Adrian at bay. He had been longing to see Halliday—and his curricle—again, and Mrs. Leigh had been forced to explain to him why that gentleman would not be calling.

After that, her family made no more mention of Travis Halliday, and Violet had heard little news of him from gossips. His sudden departure for the West Indies had been a nine-days' wonder, but since he had not left for any dramatic reason, like killing his man in a duel or eloping with the wife of a peer, speculation had died down and finally disappeared altogether.

Violet did not know whether he had married; she had half-thought that there might be some young woman in the Indies that he would take to wife, thus gaining his inheritance. And, until today, she had thought that he was still safely in the West Indies. She had worked very diligently not to think of him at all. Indeed, she often went for days now without ever hearing his laugh or seeing his face in her thoughts.

Adrian nodded, watching her uneasily. The fact that their ever-careless mother had cautioned him not to talk to Violet about Halliday had made him certain that here lay a very delicate matter. "We talked about Angelo's and Jackson's and he gave me some advice about what to do to improve my form."

He paused, but his sister said nothing. She sat very still, staring at the window.

"And he asked after everyone's health," he continued at last, "and yours most particularly."

"Very kind," she murmured.

Adrian forgot himself for a moment and grinned. "He asked after Jocko, too. Wanted to know if he'd come along to town with us."

Violet smiled briefly, but said nothing. For a minute or two, silence reigned again in the drawing room. Finally she turned and looked at him.

"Is that all you had to tell me, Adrian?"

He cleared his throat uncomfortably. "The thing is, Vi, the conversation came round to the holidays. Beaver was complaining because his family is staying in London, and he said that he had half a mind to come along with me to Ashton Park, uninvited. Just funning, of course—said he could just pretend to be a member of the family and tag along."

Another pause ensued, and Adrian attempted a brief laugh. "Halliday looked at me for a moment, then said that he supposed he would be seeing me again sooner than either of us had expected. I had no notion what he meant by that, of course, because he could have been talking about Angelo's or Tattersall's or—well, just about anywhere in town."

Violet waited patiently for Adrian to arrive at his point.

He looked at her anxiously, then said hurriedly, "The thing is, Vi, he is going to Ashton Park for Christmas, too."

Violet said nothing, merely looked away from her brother and continued to stare at the window until he got up and began to pace the room nervously.

"See here, Vi, you can't let it bother you. I know that you turned him down cold two years ago, for

Mama told me as much, but that's neither here nor there. Dash it, he's a gentleman, after all, and he will conduct himself as a gentleman should."

Violet still said nothing, so he was spurred once more into speech, trying to think of something to comfort her. "You won't have to feel uncomfortable at all when you see him again. After all, you'll have us there, too."

Finally Violet looked at him and smiled, managing to speak in quite an ordinary voice. "Please, Adrian, go and join your friends at Tattersall's. I do appreciate your telling me the news, and I shall be quite all right. Naturally I need not concern myself about seeing Mr. Halliday again."

Relieved to see that he was not to be treated to tears or sinking spells—although he knew his elder sister well enough to feel that he was quite safe from such displays—he gave her a brotherly pat on the shoulder as he departed.

"Mama's right, you know," he said encouragingly. "The house party will be great fun for all of us."

She had nodded and smiled mechanically, and Adrian had left for Tattersall's, feeling virtuously that he had done his duty.

For Violet, the peaceful solitude of the drawing room had been shattered. It had needed only this, she thought. It was not enough that she must contend with Delight Ashton and a gaggle of acquaintances and strangers, all determined to enjoy themselves. Now she had to face Travis Halliday again.

She would have preferred to set up housekeeping with Delight Ashton.

CHAPTER 7

"Well, at least the accommodations appear to be respectable," observed Fitzroy cautiously, surveying the chamber to which he had been assigned. "I am trusting, Hal, that I won't regret coming here with you."

Halliday grinned at him. "I am overcome by your desire to spend some time with a friend from whom you have been separated for the better part of two years, Fitz."

"Yes, but we could have spent that time at a number of other places that are *far* more enjoyable, Hal." Fitzroy's voice was plaintive, for it seemed to him a cruel thing to be dragged to a remote manor to spend the holidays with comparative strangers. "You still have not explained to me how you came to accept an invitation to Ashton Park. I had no notion that you and Charles Ashton were such boon companions."

"And, as ever, your powers of observation are astute, Fitz. I merely happened to run into that gentleman in White's, just after my return to civilization. He invited me to have a drink, asked me a few questions about my time in the Indies, one thing led to another, and he suggested that I spend the holidays at their house party, bringing with me any guests I wished to."

"Granting that you dropped back into the country out of the blue," Fitzroy said, walking to the window and pulling aside the drapery to see whether he had a decent view, "you still were aware that you would have been welcome any place that *I* was going for the holidays—and I did *indeed* have invitations of my own, Hal—but you did not check with me. And now we find ourselves in what could be a perfectly hideous situation with people who might well provide us with little amusement."

He turned back to his friend and raised his glass to his eye—for he had at last received a replacement from Halliday—to inspect the effect of his words. As he had suspected, they had passed over Halliday like water off a duck's back. Fitzroy forced himself to put away thoughts of Christmas at Woburn or The Priory, either of which he might have visited, certain of fashionable amusements and friends. There was no point in repining over what was not to be.

Instead, he reminded himself that he was indeed happy to see Halliday once more, and to see that all appeared to be well with his friend.

"Nonsense, Fitz! You will have a splendid time because you thrive on this sort of gathering. In no time at all you will have made yourself exceedingly comfortable and will have your group of card players established. I have full confidence in you."

"Well, just so long as there are enough respectable players—preferably some that are not ready for their last prayers—and who are amusing, as well. Since we are to be here a fortnight, I should hate to be bored witless for that period of time."

Fitzroy's valet, Briggs, entered the room just then, followed closely by a chambermaid carrying a basket of coals. She left the door slightly ajar, hurrying over to the fireplace to replenish its coals and casting a sidelong, admiring glance at the gentlemen before she bent over her work. As she bent to her task, someone else slipped into the room without being noticed.

The newcomer did not remain unnoticed for long, however. A shrill shriek from the maid and the scattering of coals across the carpet commanded the attention of everyone in the room. At first they did not see the cause of her distress but then, looking higher, they saw a monkey perched atop the highboy, his knees neatly crossed as he eyed them fastidiously through his quizzing glass, as though uncertain of whether they were worthy of associating with him.

"That's *my* quizzing glass!" exclaimed Fitzroy indignantly. "And that is the same horrid little beast that accosted us in London!"

Halliday gave a shout of laughter. "Just look at him, Fitz! He can use that glass as effectively as you do yourself—and he doesn't appear to think that we're up to his standards!"

The monkey apparently recognized Halliday's voice. He dropped his glass so that it hung from the ribbon round his neck and leaped down to Halliday's shoulder, where he proceeded to pat that gentleman on the head and pay him the compliment of carefully inspecting his hair for uninvited guests.

"Oh, I *am* sorry about the invasion!" Adrian's

head appeared around the door, and when he saw his pet, he hurried in to collect him.

Jocko chittered in protest when Adrian removed him from his friend, but Adrian remained firm. "You must stay in my chamber, Jocko!" he told the monkey firmly. "Otherwise you will land me properly in the suds."

"I had to bring him along," he informed Fitzroy and Halliday cheerfully, making his bow to them. "Brixton, our butler, informed me that he would give Mama his notice immediately if I left Jocko with him again. You didn't behave very well this last time, did you, fellow?" he said to the monkey, who shook his head in emphatic agreement.

"Brixton has my complete admiration for taking such a firm stand," said Fitzroy. "Are you saying, Mr. Leigh, that the monkey will be with us for the entire holiday?"

"Only for the part of it that I am here," replied Adrian, unperturbed by the hint that Jocko was less than welcome. "And we will be here only a fortnight."

"Splendid," said Fitzroy, his voice sinking with his spirits. He had no illusions. He looked at Jocko and saw that the monkey was watching him closely, his eyes bright and unwinking. Fitzroy was certain that when trouble came again, it would come to him. It was apparent to him that Jocko had taken him in dislike, much in the same manner that he obviously loved Halliday.

He sat down abruptly as Adrian and Jocko left the room, followed by the maid and Briggs, who closed the door carefully behind him.

"This is looking less and less like the sort of holiday I had in mind, Hal," he complained, wondering if there were some way he could make his chamber monkeyproof. Not, of course, that such a measure would keep him safe. Jocko could set upon him anywhere in the house, for he was quite certain that the boy would never be able to keep up with his pet.

"Come now, Fitz, give it time," Halliday advised him. "After all, we've only just arrived."

"Exactly," agreed Fitzroy, thinking longingly of ordering out his carriage and leaving immediately. As he gradually recovered from the shock of discovering that he would be sharing his holiday with Jocko, an unexpected thought occurred to him.

"Is Miss Leigh here, too?" he demanded, staring hard at Halliday.

Halliday met his eye easily enough. "I believe we will find that both the Misses Leigh are here," he replied calmly. "Miss Violet Leigh and her younger sister, Miss Cynthia Leigh. And their mother as well, naturally."

"Naturally," echoed Fitzroy. "Well, at least we are certain of the company of two well-bred females. I do not know how the younger one comports herself these days."

He continued to study Halliday carefully. "Have you come here because of Violet Leigh, Hal?" he asked. "Perhaps to show her again what she tossed away when she refused your offer?"

"I would scarcely be so ill-bred, Fitz," he responded. "I am shocked that you would think me capable of such behavior."

Fitzroy was unimpressed. "You know very well that you were upset with her, Hal. She overset your plans to tap into your inheritance, and she damaged your pride. You never thought that a young woman—

particularly a young woman who is not a beauty and so could expect few offers—would turn you down."

"I confess I behaved badly," admitted Halliday, turning toward the fire. "I had not considered the possibility of her refusal because we got on very well together from the first moment—and because I saw that her lot with her family was not an enviable one, and that she might welcome the freedom that I could offer her."

Fitzroy shook his head. "It won't fly, Hal. Perhaps all those things were true, but you were angry because your pride was damaged. Just think of all the young women who have dropped the handkerchief for you, yet here is one who wants none of you. You were most displeased with Miss Leigh."

"Even so, Fitz, that is not the reason that I have come here."

Fitzroy's expression indicated that he did not for a moment believe him, but he waited patiently to see what feeble excuse Halliday would present for his visit here.

"I find that I may be thinking of marriage once again, Fitz," Halliday announced, leaning back to watch his friend's reaction.

"So you *are* here because of Miss Leigh!" Fitzroy exclaimed triumphantly. "Why did you not just admit it immediately?"

"Because it is not Miss Leigh I have come to see," Halliday responded, smiling. "It is Miss Delight Ashton. I have been invited here, I gather, because Charles Ashton wishes to see if his daughter and I might suit one another. He was subtle, naturally, but I am certain that is what is on his mind."

"And you are seriously considering the match?"

Fitzroy demanded in disbelief. "Why? You no longer have any immediate need of your grandfather's fortune, do you?"

"You know that I don't, Fitz." Here his voice softened and he smiled at his companion. "I am, for the moment, well enough off. Because you stood my friend and guaranteed payment to the moneylenders, I was able to take the time I needed to set the West Indian property to rights, see a sugar cane harvest in, and to sell the land at a profit. Because of your help all is well with me once more."

Fitzroy disliked gratitude, and he moved uncomfortably, toying absently with his quizzing glass. That brought back the memory of his grievance.

"It is a thousand pities that you did not take that monkey along with you and leave him in the Indies!" he informed Halliday indignantly. "That in itself would have been worth the loan."

Halliday chuckled. "Perhaps you will come to be fond of Jocko now that you have an opportunity to become better acquainted, Fitz."

Fitzroy shuddered. "I can only hope that I need not see that wizened little face again before we leave."

The dinner gong reminded them of the time, and Halliday left to attire himself for dinner while Fitzroy submitted himself to the ministrations of Briggs. He could only hope that Jocko was safely locked away in Adrian's chamber.

CHAPTER 8

Violet dressed for dinner very carefully that evening. She knew that many of the guests had not yet arrived, but Adrian had informed her that Halliday was indeed among the early arrivals. Her heart sank, despite her brother's brisk advice to keep her chin up—and it did not help her spirits at all to learn that Adrian had brought Jocko with him. He had come up separately from the rest of the family, driving his new curricle at what he had described to his apprehensive sister as "a spanking pace." Now she was to sit down to dinner with Halliday and Delight. The holidays were not, she reflected, beginning well at all.

She muttered to herself as she finished brushing her curls into place, offering the glass her candid opinion of the manners of the undelightful Delight and the unwelcome Halliday. For the moment she refused to think about Jocko, knowing full well that she would have to think about him soon enough. His manners had not noticeably improved since coming to live with them, but he had undeniably grown attached to them, appearing to consider himself one of the family. She regretted that he had already sought out Mr. Fitzroy and could only hope that if he did any particular damage, Delight or Mr. Halliday would be the victim.

She cast a longing glance toward her bed and considered pleading a headache and having her dinner sent to her room. She could not allow herself to indulge in such craven behavior, however, and did her best to take Adrian's cheerful advice.

With her chin up, she made her way down to the drawing room, where the guests were already gathering. There were only a dozen people or so, and the gentlemen had positioned themselves in front of the fire. She saw Halliday immediately, standing out from the other men as it seemed to her he always did. He looked very much at ease, and she saw that his months in the West Indies sun had darkened his skin so that his eyes seemed to shine even more brightly than she remembered.

She was dismayed to have him look up and catch her eye. *How horrid, how pitiful,* she scolded herself, *to have been caught looking at him.* Nonetheless, she smiled pleasantly and allowed not a nerve to show.

"Why, Miss Leigh! What a pleasure it is to see you again!" he said, leaving the fire and walking toward her. She would have sworn that his tone and manner were sincere, but then she knew him to be the master of the polished address. He had probably already spoken in the same tone to Delight, who was hovering next to Mrs. Ashton and watching Violet's entrance like a hawk.

Violet dropped him a brief curtsey and smiled as bland a smile as she could muster, but before she could reply, Delight, who had been listening intently, decided to contribute her mite to the conversation.

"Yes, it *is* rather hard to miss poor Violet when

she enters a room, is it not?" she trilled, her giggle as irritating as it had always been. She hurried over to tuck her arm through Violet's, quite as though they were truly old friends and as though she were merely teasing instead of holding Violet up to ridicule. "She has always towered over the rest of us—she has *always* been a full head higher than I, even when we were in the nursery."

Here she looked up at Halliday through thick eyelashes. "We have always been as unlike as posies and potatoes!"

A brief glint showed in Halliday's eyes at this sally, and he glanced appreciatively at Violet. "Yes, I can see that is quite true, Miss Ashton," he assured her.

Before Delight could capitalize upon her moment, Fitzroy separated himself from the other men and joined them, bowing to Violet.

"I am also very glad to see you again, Miss Leigh," he said, and his sincerity was so unmistakable that Violet had no trouble at all in smiling at him.

"And I to see you, Mr. Fitzroy." She looked at him and shook her head lightly. "I fear that I must already apologize once more for Jocko. I believe that he must seek you out deliberately."

Fitzroy, who shared much the same notion, nodded, trying to keep the signs of incipient panic from his expression at the mention of his nemesis.

"Who is Jocko?" asked Delight, both puzzled and irritated at being suddenly excluded from the conversation.

"Oh, Jocko is Adrian's monkey!" announced Mrs. Leigh, who had entered the drawing room just in time to hear her question. "I am afraid, Deidre, that you will have an extra guest in Jocko, but I promise you that he will be kept *very* carefully in his cage. You shall not even know he is here!"

She spoke with such absolute confidence that Mrs. Ashton accepted her friend's guarantee at face value and assured her that they were more than happy to welcome Jocko for the festivities.

"Monkeys are such amusing creatures, are they not?" she said, smiling vaguely at the group in general.

There was an equally vague murmur of agreement, but Fitzroy did not lend his voice to it. He looked pale and his hunted expression had returned. He did not share Mrs. Leigh's comfortable confidence in Adrian's ability to keep Jocko contained.

Seeing Fitzroy's face, Halliday chuckled and glanced toward Violet, whose eyes were also alight with amusement. They enjoyed the moment but then, remembering their present circumstances, each quickly looked away to become occupied with another guest and another conversation.

Dinner was all that Violet had feared it would be, and she was not consoled to think that the next day was Christmas Eve. This was her favorite holiday of the year, and she was spending it in circumstances that were the least conducive to her happiness. She watched Delight flirt with Mr. Halliday while she herself made polite conversation with Fitzroy, who was her dinner partner, and carefully avoided the worried glances that Adrian kept shooting her way. While his concern for her welfare was gratifying, it was already beginning to wear.

Surveying the group, she was grateful to see that none of the guests that had appeared thus far offered any particular threat to her peace of mind where Adrian and Cynthia were concerned. A Mr. and Mrs. Dinsdale, a comfortably middle-aged couple fond of cribbage, and Mrs. Shaw, an elderly neighbor who had driven over for the occasion, were the only ones present apart from the two families, Halliday, and Fitzroy. Since Delight had clearly marked Mr. Halliday as her own, he would, she hoped, not become a target of Cynthia's exercises in flirtation, and Fitzroy was too much the gentleman to offer a threat. Halliday's presence might, of course, encourage Adrian to gamble, but she felt that she would be able to take care of that problem should it arise.

Her satisfaction was destroyed, however, when she heard Mrs. Ashton speak. Apparently feeling that Adrian looked a little depressed by his company—which was true, for he had just been wondering how he would endure a fortnight in such company—she attempted to cheer him.

"No need to fall into the dismals, Adrian," she assured him. "Tomorrow we expect a positive flood of guests, and one or two of them are particular friends of yours, I believe—Nathan Lamb and William Delaney."

Adrian brightened immediately, but his sister's heart sank. Both of those young men had also been sent down from university for much the same behavior as Adrian. That was all he needed: encouragement to behave badly. She would have to be very alert, and very mindful of Cynthia, who would care for nothing except enjoying herself and would give not a thought to how her behavior might affect her reputation and the season that she was about to embark upon in London. Mrs. Leigh, she knew, would be oblivious to it all, happy as long as her children were enjoying themselves.

When the ladies retired to the drawing room, Violet saw that the evening was going to be interminable. She found a quiet corner from which she could observe the others peacefully, but Delight sought her out immediately, eager to speak of Travis Halliday. To her faint amusement, Delight spoke of him as though he were her latest conquest.

"Mr. Halliday is just now back from the West Indies," she informed Violet airily. "He has substantial holdings there, you know—or at least he did until he sold them recently."

"Indeed," murmured Violet, hoping to appear indifferent enough that Delight would find a different topic.

She was unsuccessful, however, for Delight found her subject too appealing to abandon.

"I was astonished when he wished to come here for the holidays, so soon after his return to England," Delight continued, attempting to look prettily unconscious of the implied compliment to herself, "but my father said that when he offered Mr. Halliday the invitation to Ashton Park, he replied that he could think of *nothing* he wished to do more than come here to us."

Violet could not decide just what to say to this, so she responded with a polite smile.

"I believe that some people thought that he was mildly taken with you, Violet, just before he left the country . . . but then, he *did* leave, did he not?"

Violet, not pleased with the direction the conversation was taking, nonetheless felt that she could safely agree with Delight about the latter part of her observation, so she nodded.

"Yes, Mr. Halliday *did* indeed leave, and has been gone for quite some time. I daresay he must find it strange here, after being so long away," she added, hoping to turn Delight's thoughts in another direction.

"I know that *some* people were disposed to believe that he paid you marked attention just before leaving, Violet, but then I have always admired gentlemen who are kind to ladies who have no other partners."

"What a rapper, Delight! You know that Vi had all the partners she needed at that ball—*and* that Halliday made her the talk of the evening because he danced only with her and then had supper with her!"

Adrian had entered the drawing room slightly in advance of the other gentlemen, and he and Cynthia had strolled over to Violet just in time to hear Delight's remark.

Delight flushed an unbecoming lobster-red and glared at Adrian. "What would you know about it?" she demanded. "You weren't even present that evening!"

"No, but our mother was, and she gave Cyn and me a glowing description of the whole matter the next morning—after Halliday came to call and took Vi out in his curricle."

This final memory turned his train of thought immediately. "You know, I tried to find a curricle just like that one when I purchased mine, but I couldn't find one. You remember, Vi, that it had silver molding, and its lamps and swordcase were handsomer than mine."

He looked mildly discontented as he mulled that over. "Still, mine is handsome enough—even Freddie says so, and no one has a more practiced eye than he does—and the pair of bays I bought are outstanding!"

Seeing the other gentlemen at last entering the room, he excused himself to hurry over to Halliday and regale him with the finer points of his new cattle, certain of an interested listener.

Violet murmured that she believed her mother was in need of her and made a hasty escape, abandoning Cynthia to the company of Delight, who had been rendered momentarily speechless, both by Adrian's attack and by the news that Violet had ridden in Mr. Halliday's curricle.

Violet appreciated her brother's defense of her, but she knew that he had only made things more difficult, for now Delight would be angry enough to search for other ways in which to make her miserable.

She was mildly comforted when Mr. Fitzroy intercepted her, and they exchanged a few polite remarks about London events, giving her the opportunity to discuss impersonal matters and restore her equanimity. By the time Halliday joined them, she was quite herself again, and managed to see the evening through to its end without further difficulties. It was with the deepest gratitude that she took her candle to go upstairs and put the day behind her.

CHAPTER 9

Morning brought its comfort, but only until Violet awakened enough to remember where she was. Her first thoughts were cheerful, for it was Christmas Eve and today they would be gathering greens to decorate the house. This was one of her favorite activities of the year, for she loved the bustle of going out to collect them and the beauty of the greenery and its symbolism of life continuing even during the bleakness of winter. Then she recalled that she would not be decorating Richland, but Ashton Park—and that her company would be quite a different group from the usual one at home.

She sat up crossly and threw back the covers, startling the maid who was tending the fire and not expecting her to be awake so early. Perhaps they did not even decorate at Ashton Park, she thought. Perhaps their idea of Christmas began and ended with collecting a captive audience for the holidays. Perhaps last night was a foretaste of the entire experience.

That was not, she scolded herself, a particularly charitable attitude toward her hosts. Delight, of course, was and always had been a thorn in her side, but her parents were pleasant—if somewhat bland—

people. Still, she had not been even a full day at Ashton and already she had been subjected to several of Mr. Ashton's stories. They were harmless, but extraordinarily boring, and he paused regularly and looked at his listener so expectantly that one was obligated to make a response of some sort. The stories were also, with few exceptions, much the same ones that he had been telling for years. He considered himself a raconteur, but that belief was very wide of the mark.

Violet shivered as she hurried toward the fire to dress for the morning. Determined to enjoy the day despite her situation, she chose a scarlet sash to wear with her dark morning gown, and caught up her curls with ribbons of the same color. Her choice, she told herself firmly, had nothing to do with Mr. Halliday and everything to do with the season. Humming "The Holly and the Ivy," she went cheerfully down to the dining room, expecting to have it to herself because of the early hour. It was very likely that the others would not stir for hours. She would undoubtedly have time for a walk in the brisk early morning and some time to read in peace next to the drawing-room fire.

"Good morning, Miss Leigh. I had not thought to have a companion at breakfast." Mr. Halliday was standing at the sideboard, serving his plate, as she entered the dining room. "How much more pleasant to have your company than to dine alone."

Violet placed no stock at all in his words. She was certain that he wished her in Hades rather than here with him. She knew that he had not been pleased by her rejection of his offer, but his polished manner would not allow him to be truthful. Uncomfortably, she murmured something inconsequential to his pleasantry, served her plate, and sat down at table with him. She could not seat herself so far away as she wished, but she at least placed herself so that she need not catch his eye each time she looked up. Instead, a large window gave a view of the park, with a handsome stand of oaks rising in the distance. She wondered for a moment if they would gather greenery there—or if indeed they would do so at all.

"I saw from your family's manner last night that you have visited Ashton Park before," he remarked after a few minutes had passed in silence.

"Yes," she responded, hoping that she would not convey her feeling about that unhappy fact in her tone. "Mrs. Ashton and my mother were girlhood friends, so we have come here a number of times over the years, and they have been to Richland."

Before he could comment further, she decided to return the ball to his court. She had no wish to discuss her relationship with the Ashtons, but she was most certainly curious about his time away from England. She had expected to hear that he had married straightaway and thus gained access to the fortune he needed, but that obviously had not happened. She was interested in Delight's information about his family's holdings in the West Indies and what he had done while living there.

From time to time she had wondered if she had given too much weight to the words of Lady Dismore and Mrs. Digby. On the whole, though, she thought she had been quite correct in her decision. Even if some of their information about Mr. Halliday had been slightly melodramatic, she had learned from the gossip of the *ton* that he was indeed a gambler, which would not suit her, and that he was fond of colorful love affairs. She had seen Anna Aubrey, too, and had known at a glance that she and that lady had nothing in common. Miss Aubrey was a very pretty, very petite blonde, certain of her many attractions. Violet knew that the real reason she had not been able to accept Travis Halliday's offer was that she had been deeply drawn to him, while he had seen her merely as a handy means to an end. That she could never have borne. Far better, she thought, to marry someone for whom she felt no strong attachment. There would be far less risk for her in such a marriage.

She hoped that none of her thoughts showed in her face as she turned the conversation. "I understand that you have recently returned from the West Indies, Mr. Halliday," she said. "It must seem very strange to be back in England, in such a completely different climate."

"You are certainly correct that it is a very different climate, Miss Leigh," he conceded, "but I have been back long enough to become accustomed to English weather and English ways. I arrived several weeks ago."

"Indeed? I had understood that you were newly come from the Indies." It would be a great disappointment to Delight if she were to learn that he had not rushed from the ship to Ashton Park, but she had no intention of raising the subject. Still, she had noticed that Mr. Fitzroy seemed to share the same impression of his friend's recent arrival.

"I went first to Bellington, which is my home," he replied. "I had a number of business affairs to settle there before going on to London."

Violet nodded absently, watching a distant rider through the window. "You must have been very glad to see it once again. You have been long away."

She flushed after saying this, for she did not wish to make him think that she had been considering how long he had been away, nor that she had been thinking of his proposal.

"Yes, it has seemed a very long time indeed," he answered, looking at her directly. She felt his gaze upon her and reluctantly turned her eyes from the window to meet his, not wishing to seem rude. "I was more than glad to see Bellington again, and to feel English soil beneath my feet once more."

"I am certain that is true," she said, forcing herself to smile. "I have never traveled away from this country myself, but I know that I am eager enough to return to Richland after merely being away in London for several weeks."

After a very brief pause, curiosity overcame her and she added, "I trust that you accomplished all that you had hoped to while you were away, sir. It would seem a hardship indeed to be separated so long from your home to no purpose."

"I thank you for your concern, ma'am," he replied. "I am happy to say that I did accomplish all that was needed."

Violet could see that he had no intention of being more forthcoming with information about his trip or about his purpose for making the journey, so, not wishing to seem too inquisitive, she brought up the other subject that occupied her thoughts this morning.

She nodded toward the stand of oaks in the distance. "I have been wondering whether we will be going to gather greenery today," she said, her voice deliberately light. "And, if we are, whether we will be walking in that direction."

He turned to gaze out the window and smiled. "I had quite forgotten that today is Christmas Eve. It has been a good many years since I went out to search for evergreens to decorate the hall. I haven't done so since I was a boy and both my parents were still alive."

"I love the tradition. We have done so every year since I was very small." Violet smiled sincerely as she said this, remembering their forays into the neighborhood spinneys to search for greens.

"Brixton always drove a pony-cart for us, and as soon as Adrian was old enough, he took the ribbons of a second one." She sighed. "I told Brixton to be certain to go out for the greenery today and to decorate the house just as he would if the family were present. The staff looks forward to that, too."

"And just who is Brixton?" Halliday inquired curiously.

"Our butler. He has been a part of Richland for forty years. Brixton came as a footman when my father was just a boy."

"And it was the long-suffering Brixton that informed your brother that he would not keep Jocko for the holidays?"

Violet laughed. "Yes. I cannot blame him in the least. Even though Jocko has a very pleasant room of his own next to the conservatory and is supposed to come out only when one of us is attending him, he inevitably escapes and creates chaos wherever he goes. He has a most inquiring nature."

"I have noticed that. And does Jocko accompany

you and your family in your holiday tradition of searching for greenery? And assist in decorating, of course?"

"Redecorating would be closer to the truth," Violet said, remembering last Christmas with a slight shudder. "He apparently did not care for the way in which we had arranged things. But even that couldn't spoil the fun."

She sighed a little, recalling past Christmases. "I wish that we were at Richland. We would spend all afternoon looking for our holly and ivy."

"And mistletoe," added Halliday.

She nodded, laughing. "And mistletoe, of course. Adrian once climbed up into the highest part of a lime tree to retrieve a bunch of mistletoe—only to come tumbling all the way to the ground. He terrified us and broke his leg; Brixton had to carry him back to the cart. But Adrian had the mistletoe clutched in his arms and he wouldn't let go of it. We had our kissing bough."

Halliday chuckled. "He seems a most determined young man."

"So he is," she agreed wholeheartedly, "although headstrong is sometimes another word for it."

A series of piercing shrieks ended their conversation. They stared at one another for a moment, then rose and hurried toward the stairs, abandoning their breakfasts. They were joined on the stairway by the butler and two footmen, all of them rushing in the same direction, all of them prepared to see that, at the very least, a murder had been committed.

In the wing of family bedrooms on the next floor, they saw Delight in the passage, attired in her nightgown, her hair tumbled over shaking shoulders. With her were her parents, both of them in their dressing gowns, along with Mrs. Leigh, Adrian, and Mr. Fitzroy. Clearly, all of them had been awakened from a sound sleep, and Adrian, who was convulsed with laughter, was holding Jocko.

"You should see yourself, Delight!" he chortled. "You look the most complete pea-goose! And all over one small monkey!"

It was, Violet reflected, probably not the wisest response Adrian could have made to Delight's distress, but she could scarcely blame him. There was a certain satisfaction in seeing smugness gone all to pieces.

Delight's complexion grew an even more unpleasant shade of red at Adrian's words—and at the realization that Mr. Halliday and Mr. Fitzroy were also present.

"This was undoubtedly your doing!" she exclaimed, turning on the unwary Violet. "Did you put this monkey into my chamber?"

"Come now, Delight! Don't be paper-skulled!" pleaded Adrian. "Jocko stays with me, not with Vi. And he did you no harm, after all."

"No harm?" she retorted. "No harm to be awakened and see a small, wizened, *ugly* face staring down at me? No harm to nearly faint dead away with fear?"

"Anyone who can scream like that was not about to faint!" Adrian responded. "And Jocko is *not* ugly! He is an excessively handsome animal! Everyone says so!"

Jocko, who was perched on his master's shoulder, chittered his agreement.

"What Delight needs is a cup of tea and a little peace and quiet to regain her composure," said Violet, giving her brother a warning glance. Now was not the time to take up the cudgels in Jocko's behalf.

"What Delight needs," said that lady in a quivering voice, "is to have all of you go about your business and leave me *alone!*" She turned and stormed into her chamber, slamming the door behind her.

Slowly the rest of them began to drift away, Mr. Ashton returning to his chamber and Mrs. Ashton going hesitantly into her daughter's to attempt to comfort her. Experience had taught her that this would be a difficult task.

"Really, dearest, you *must* keep Jocko under lock and key." Mrs. Leigh looked at her son reproachfully. "I promised Deirdre *faithfully* that you would do so."

"And I am doing my best, Mama!" Adrian protested. "But you know how clever he is. I daresay Jocko can open the door himself—and I don't wish to put him into his travel cage. Besides, Cyn will only let him out again if I do."

Mrs. Leigh nodded regretfully, then turned back to her own room, putting the matter entirely from her mind. Adrian turned to his sister and grinned.

"Quite a sight, wasn't it, Vi?" he murmered quietly. "I daresay Delight will think once or twice before she takes potshots at you as she did last night."

"Did you *deliberately* put Jocko in her chamber, Adrian?" Violet whispered urgently. "You should not have done so. You know very well that this will only make things worse."

"She was going to be a terror come what may, Vi. You know that." Adrian was unrepentant. "But now you have a little of your own back again. Wasn't it great sport to see her? It was almost as good as that summer when I smeared honey inside her bonnet!"

Chortling, he and Jocko made their way back to the safety of their chamber, Adrian patting his pet approvingly.

Fitzroy's eyes were closed and he shook his head. "That could have been me," he murmured. "I might have awakened eyeball-to-eyeball with that little beast."

"But you did not, Fitz," Halliday reminded him. "You must look at the bright side of matters. Miss Ashton bore the brunt of Jocko's attention, and now that he knows the way to her chamber, perhaps you and she will share his attentions."

Fitzroy's eyes flew open. "You know, Hal, I realize that it isn't the most gentlemanly thing to say, but I would be delighted to share the monkey's attentions with her. And you are absolutely correct! I hadn't thought at all that this might take the focus away from me. I daresay that there are many more interesting things in her chamber than in mine."

Greatly comforted by this thought, Fitzroy left them, telling Halliday that since he had been awakened at this barbaric hour he would dress and come down for breakfast shortly.

"Shortly means two hours," Halliday informed Violet as they returned to their breakfasts. "Briggs does not allow his master to leave the chamber until he is a work of art."

Violet smiled and thought briefly of the few minutes it had taken her to complete her own toilette without benefit of a lady's maid. She finished her breakfast quickly, made her excuses to Halliday as he prepared to await his friend, and went out for a solitary ramble to enjoy the glories of a Christmas Eve morning.

CHAPTER 10

By the time Violet had returned from her walk and spent a little time with her book beside the fire, new guests were beginning to arrive. Somewhat to her dismay, Nathan Lamb and William Delaney were among the first to appear, arriving together in a burst of energy and bonhomie that was almost overwhelming. Adrian and Cynthia were delighted to see them, and the four of them disappeared into the billiards room as soon as the young men had seen their luggage settled in the chamber they would share.

Violet sighed. She was going to earn Cynthia's deepest disapproval, but she knew that she was going to have to watch her younger sister like a hawk to be certain that she did nothing foolish. She decided that she could allow Cynthia a little while in the billiards room, but soon she would have to extract her from that masculine sanctuary. She would have to do so immediately if any unknown gentlemen decided to join the billiards party.

The rest of the morning was filled with the sound of crunching gravel as carriages filled with guests pulled up to the main door, and Violet retreated to a secluded corner of the drawing room. She watched with interest as the newcomers swept by and up the stairs to the guest chambers, guided assiduously by what seemed like a fleet of footmen and maids. As she watched the parade pass by, she marveled that there could be chambers for so many people. Ashton Park was of generous size, but she had not dreamed that it could house so many.

Mrs. Leigh and Mrs. Ashton came down soon after the last influx of guests, and Mrs. Leigh informed Violet happily that a group would be going out shortly to gather the greenery.

"Violet *adores* this part of Christmas," Mrs. Leigh told her friend. "It is dearer to her than almost any other part of the season."

Even though that was true, Violet hated to hear her mother talking about her in such a manner. Hearing her own feelings exposed always made her feel vulnerable—and, in this case, quite childish as well. Besides, she wanted to shout that she loved that part of Christmas at home, but they were *not* at home; she very well might not like the way it was done at Ashton Park.

Being well-bred, however, she restrained herself and waited to see how matters would develop. At least she could go out by herself and collect some greens for her own chamber. That could offend no one, and she would be able to carry out the ritual just as she pleased.

However, she soon discovered that there was to be a major outing. New guests had drifted down to the drawing room, and Mr. Ashton appeared to announce that anyone who wished to join the party searching for evergreens should don warm coats and sturdy boots and assemble in the entryway.

Fitzroy looked horrified at the mention of sturdy boots and cast an anguished glance at his own highly-polished Hessians, then announced his firm intention of retiring to the library to read the newspaper. Two or three other gentlemen favored his suggestion, and most of the ladies, including Mrs. Leigh and Mrs. Ashton, said that they also would remain at the house.

Violet had thought that Delight might not wish to trek through the fields and woodland, but her hopes were dashed when Delight smiled brightly at Mr. Halliday, saying that there was nothing she enjoyed more than this Christmas ritual. Violet knew from personal experience that Delight objected to any activity that might muss her hair or her clothing and did not believe her for a second, but Mr. Halliday merely returned Delight's smile and agreed that there were few things more pleasant than this old-fashioned ceremony.

Led by Mr. Ashton, a group of about a dozen mostly young people assembled in the entryway. Introductions were made, and Violet was pleased to see that there was another young woman just Cynthia's age who would also have her coming-out in the spring. At least there would be someone to keep her company, so that Violet might prevent her from being always with Adrian and his friends.

Aside from those individuals and Mr. Ashton, the party was comprised of Delight, Mr. Halliday, and five people that she had just met: a young married couple, Mr. and Mrs. Frederick Haynes; a spinster cousin of Deirdre Ashton, Miss Olivia Thaxton; and two other single gentlemen, Mr. Arthur Randall and Mr. Terence Agnew.

Mr. Randall sought Violet's company as they set off across the park, inquiring with genuine interest about her family, her home, and her usual holiday activities.

"I am afraid I am very much an interloper here," he explained cheerfully. "I found myself at loose ends in London, and Charles Ashton had been kind enough to tell me to come along here for the holidays if I wished to do so. So, here I am, a last-minute guest, dropping in out of the blue. I am certain that Mrs. Ashton must wish me anywhere but here."

"I am equally certain that she wishes no such thing," Violet assured him, smiling. "Every hostess must be glad to have a well-mannered, intelligent young gentleman as her guest. You are a commodity in great demand, sir. Pray do not underestimate your value."

He gave her a brief bow. "You are very kind, Miss Leigh, but I am nonetheless certain that my unannounced arrival must be an imposition. I had thought I would remain in the city, but I found at the last moment that I did not wish to be alone during the holidays."

"Does your family live far away, Mr. Randall?" she inquired, wondering why he should be alone.

He shook his head. "I am afraid that I find myself without a family, Miss Leigh," he responded. "My parents died long ago, and the elderly uncle that I lived with died last spring."

"I am very sorry to hear that, sir, and I am sorry that I brought up a subject that must be painful to you."

He shook his head and smiled at her reassuringly.

"I have grown accustomed to the thought of being alone—or at least I thought I had until we came closer to the holiday season. I find it is a pleasure to be with others in a busy household instead of dining alone."

"Well, if you wished for a busy household, you most certainly have had your wish granted," she said cheerfully, glancing at the group around them.

Adrian and his companions had paused to reenact, briefly but loudly, a hunting scene in which they had participated that fall and in which they had all acquitted themselves extremely well. Cynthia and Miss Langley, the newcomer her own age, were watching them with appreciative amusement. Mr. Agnew was strolling along with Mr. and Mrs. Haynes, while Mr. Ashton was recounting one of his many stories for the benefit of Miss Thaxton, his wife's cousin. Delight was clinging to Mr. Halliday's arm as though she feared she might slip and fall and looking up at him as she talked, her mouth curved in a satisfied smile.

On the whole, Violet was very glad to have been singled out by Mr. Randall. He was very easy to talk with and it was with surprise that she realized they had been talking for some time. They had passed the stand of oaks some time ago and climbed a gentle hill that stretched away to a wooded area behind a stone wall.

"Yes, they all appear very animated, don't they? Your brother, in particular, seems very lively," Mr. Randall responded. "I should imagine there will be few dull moments during the next fortnight."

Violet, her thoughts diverted for the moment to the abandoned Jocko, nodded in agreement. She hoped the little monkey was safely in his cage; if not, they would return to more unpleasant scenes. The next two weeks stretched before her like a vast desert, offering little in the way of an oasis. Only the company of Mr. Randall seemed to offer her any respite.

"Yes, Adrian is indeed very high-spirited," she agreed a little dryly. "One can never be certain what he will do next."

They had come to a stile, and the group slowed as the ladies were helped over the stone wall. Beyond it they could see a grove of trees, and Mr. Ashton assured them that just beyond that grove they would find some very fine holly bushes. He had sent a servant 'round by the road, driving a cart in which they could place their gleanings.

As promised, the group discovered there a fine, thick hedge of holly bushes, their berries bright in the winter sunlight. The cart had already arrived, and the servant dispensed shears and heavy gloves to the gentlemen, so that they could cut the branches of holly, and baskets to the ladies to collect them. Adrian and his friends were more disposed to frolic than to gather holly, but the others labored diligently under Mr. Ashton's supervision.

As the cart slowly filled with greenery, they paused for the refreshments that the servant had brought with him. To Violet's amusement, the food was set out on a pair of folding campaign tables, which had been covered with a fine linen cloth. The food was simple but plentiful: sandwiches and fruit, coffee and cakes. Violet discovered that the brisk air had given her a healthy appetite, and she was enjoying a second sandwich when she heard Mr. Halliday's voice.

"You are looking remarkably well today, Miss Leigh," he said. "Did you choose the scarlet ribbons with a view to matching the holly berries?"

"How discerning you are, sir," she replied. "I naturally had that in mind. Rarely do I wear this color except when I expect to be close to a holly bush . . . or perhaps to a rose garden, if it has roses of this particular shade."

He nodded, his expression serious but his eyes smiling. "It is always best to plan carefully. I also try to plan my wardrobe according to the setting in which I know I shall find myself. I should not wish to be guilty of clashing. I have been associated with Mr. Fitzroy for too long to make such an egregious error."

Violet chuckled at this accurate portrayal of Fitzroy's obsession with his wardrobe and appearance, but Delight, who had been standing close to Halliday during this exchange, frowned at them.

"Whatever are you talking about?" she demanded. "That sounds like the sheerest foolishness to me."

"And so it is," Violet agreed. "The whole matter of wardrobe is a completely frivolous one." She took another bite of her sandwich, enjoying the sight of the green holly bushes decorated with their glossy berries.

"It is no wonder that you have grown to be such an amazon, Violet," Delight observed. "You have always had the most astounding appetite."

She looked up appealingly at Mr. Halliday. "I can scarcely bring myself to eat a crumb during the day. My mother has always worried about me because I have such an amazingly tiny appetite. She has feared that I will be taken ill."

Violet, remembering one night at Miss Delaware's Academy when Delight had eaten half of a cake brought to one of the other girls as a special treat and then become most horribly sick, laughed.

"Yes, Delight, and so she should worry! Do you remember the cake that Lydia Burnham's grandmother brought to her? As I recall, you did become quite ill!" Violet said nothing more, but her eyes were dancing.

Delight stiffened and her color rose. "I have always been delicate, as you know very well, Violet Leigh!" She turned hastily and walked to the table, where she selected one of the cakes and bit into it daintily. She took only a single bite, then set down her plate on the table—a clear indication to anyone watching that she survived on a diet of dewdrops and bread crumbs.

Violet, catching sight of some ivy in a low-growing bush in the nearby grove, gave no more thought to Delight. Taking a basket and a pair of shears, she strolled toward her quarry, prepared to occupy herself with more enjoyable subjects.

Before Mr. Randall could move to follow her, Halliday had already joined her, shears in hand, plucking up a fine strand of ivy.

"You quite overset Miss Ashton," he observed, snipping carefully.

"It would appear so," she responded, "but she will recover quickly. She always does."

"I take it that this pulling of caps is quite a common thing for the two of you."

"Ever since I can remember," agreed Violet. "And it shows no signs of abating. I believe that the best way to deal with it is for me to keep my distance." She sighed. "Unfortunately, since my mother and Mrs. Ashton are such bosom bows, there is no chance of that—so here I am."

"All is not lost, however. You and Randall appear to be getting along famously." His voice was casual, but she glanced at him quickly. He was studiously measuring the next strand of ivy, his attention apparently deeply absorbed by that undertaking.

"Yes, he is very much the gentleman," she said. "Are you acquainted with him?"

"Yes, he seems a good enough sort," Halliday admitted, holding the ivy out the length of his arm.

"He told me that he has no family, and so he decided to accept Mr. Ashton's invitation here for Christmas."

"Yes, he and I have that much in common, at least." He mused over his work before adding, "I had heard that he was once briefly engaged, but it did not last."

"That is a pity," said Violet sincerely. "He seems a lonely man, and a marriage could provide him with companionship."

"Perhaps the lady in question was not the right companion for him," persisted Halliday. "In that case, the union would not have been a happy one."

"True," Violet agreed. "But if the young lady was sensible and kind and there was not too great an attachment between them, then they would very likely have made a successful marriage."

At this he turned abruptly to stare at her. "And so you think that those qualities are all they need to have in common?" he demanded.

She nodded. "Except very likely only one of them

needs to be sensible, if they both are kind. If they have that much, they will go on together very well."

Halliday gave up all pretense of collecting ivy to stare at her. "That seems a strangely cold view of marriage for a young woman to have, Miss Leigh. You quite astonish me!"

Violet laughed. "I am certain that astonishing you must be one of my greater feats, Mr. Halliday. I feel quite puffed up in my own esteem."

"Are you saying, Miss Leigh, that you yourself would marry under the circumstances you just described?"

She looked at him squarely, not allowing herself so much as a blink. "If I should decide to marry, sir, you may be assured that I would not consider any other circumstances."

Rising quickly, she took her basket and returned to the cart, where Mr. Randall soon rejoined her. Delight, seeing Mr. Halliday at liberty once more, took his arm and drew him down a woodland path, glancing back to throw Violet a triumphant look.

CHAPTER 11

When the bed of the cart was finally filled to the brim with greenery, the group started back, taking a detour by way of the apple orchard. The apple trees would supply them with mistletoe and their afternoon's work would be complete. Mr. Ashton carried a bag with him, and they deposited several bunches within it, then turned gratefully toward Ashton Park, looking forward to a warm fire and dinner.

As they approached the main door of the house, it was thrown open and Fitzroy appeared, white-faced and tense. Violet watched apprehensively as he hurried toward Mr. Halliday and took him to one side. She was certain that Jocko had taken advantage of their absence to call upon Mr. Fitzroy once more.

"You will *not* credit what has happened here this afternoon, Hal!" he said in a voice that was kept deliberately low but was nonetheless pulsing with emotion. "I can scarcely credit it myself!"

"Well, Fitz, go ahead and tell me your news, and perhaps you will be able to believe it then."

Fitzroy looked at him resentfully. "Well, I assure

you that you would not take it lightly had it happened to *you*, Hal!"

"Had what happened to me, Fitz? I have not the least notion what you are speaking of."

The rest of the group had gone on into the house, eager to freshen up and rest in front of a warm fire or to retire once more to the billiards room. Only Violet and Delight noticed that Fitzroy and Halliday were still outside.

"I am being forced to *share* my chamber, Hal!" he announced, his tone the same that one would use if announcing an approaching execution.

Halliday grinned at him. "I had no notion it was something so serious, Fitz. You should have warned me to sit down first."

"Most amusing! Now ask me with *whom* I am to share my chamber!"

"Very well," responded Halliday indulgently. "With *whom* are you being forced to share your chamber?"

"Crawton!" replied Fitzroy, his voice quivering with indignation. "I am to be obliged to share a chamber with *Basil Crawton!*"

He saw that he finally had his friend's attention and relaxed slightly. "You see, Hal! I *told* you would not be able to credit the news!"

"What is Crawton doing here?" inquired Halliday, frowning.

"My question precisely," Fitzroy returned, pleased to see that they were in agreement. "When I asked him, he informed me that Ashton is a distant relative of his—a second cousin, twice removed, or some such cock-and-bull tale! He well may be some sort of relation, but I believe that he is here because no one else will have him and he would be pursued by duns in London—or perhaps he is unable to go to any of his gambling haunts because he has failed to meet a debt of honor!"

Only a moment's reflection was required to convince Halliday of the probable truth of Fitzroy's evaluation of the situation.

"Still, Fitz," he said, shaking his head, "there is nothing we can do about it. He is Ashton's guest just as we are, and we must treat him as such."

Fitzroy found small comfort in this view, but was at last consoled by Halliday's guarantee that he could move in with him rather than share a chamber with the detestable Crawton.

"Unless, of course, they now have Jocko residing with *me*," Halliday added. "You know how crowded it can become at a house party."

Fitzroy dismissed his remark as unworthy of comment and hurried to tell Briggs the glad tidings that he was to move his master's belongings to a more suitable habitation.

To Violet's pleasure, Mr. Randall escorted her in to dinner that evening. Delight, naturally, had arranged to have Mr. Halliday as her partner.

Watching her cling to Halliday's arm as they paraded into the dining room caused Adrian to inform Cynthia in a low voice that Delight looked like a cat at the cream pot. "Just as though he would pay any notice to her!" he said in disgust.

Fortunately for Adrian, however, he had his mother's happy nature, and his moment of irritation was soon dissipated as he turned to exchange a comment with Delaney and to offer his arm to Miss Langley, who was to be his partner at dinner.

The group at table that night was far different from the more sedate group of the previous evening. The gathering was now three times larger and the mood as many times lighter. The merriment provided by Adrian and his companions permeated the atmosphere, and everyone—even Delight—seemed disposed to enjoy themselves.

The gentlemen did not linger at the table after dinner because everyone was preparing to hang the greenery, or at least to watch it being hung and to help direct the activity. Violet had Cynthia and Miss Langley busily putting together the kissing boughs, and lengths of gold and crimson ribbons shone brightly in the candlelight.

"How long ago it all seems," sighed Mrs. Leigh as she watched the girls at work.

"How long ago what seems, dear lady?" inquired Mr. Chesterton, the most recent addition to the party, who had been her partner at dinner. He had met Mrs. Leigh only hours ago, and had already fallen prey to her charm.

"When I was their age and making my first kissing bough." Her smile was gentle and her voice soft, and poor Mr. Chesterton had not a prayer of resisting her. "It seems as though it all belonged to another world."

"Don't speak as though you are old, ma'am," he begged her. "You look as though you should be seated with the young ladies now, not over here with those of us who have grown older. By some magical charm, you have remained bewitchingly young, Mrs. Leigh. I cannot imagine how you manage it."

Violet, standing near enough to overhear this exchange, could not repress a smile. Her mother was really quite incorrigible. She could no sooner resist a flirtation than a bird could resist flying. It was her natural inclination, and she did it so gracefully and naturally that she could never be accused of playing anyone false. She felt from the heart whatever she said—but she might feel it for only a very few minutes.

Violet abandoned Mr. Chesterton to his fate and returned to help the girls with their work. She could hear Adrian's shouts from the entry hall as he and Delaney attempted to arrange a wreath some twenty feet above them, aided by an intrepid footman. Mr. Ashton seemed cheerfully oblivious to the uproar—and the endangerment of his household—as the decorating progressed.

Fitzroy had overseen a tasteful arrangement on the mantel of the drawing room fireplace and had then arranged himself comfortably in front of it to appreciate his handiwork. No sooner had he settled himself, however, than Lord Crawton appeared next to him.

"Sorry to have chased you out of your room, Fitzroy," he said amiably, his dark eyes showing his amusement.

Fitzroy sat up as though galvanized, but, remembering that they were both Ashton's guests, maintained his calm. "Not a problem, I assure you," he replied stiffly. "There is more space for me in Halliday's chamber."

Crawton nodded, knowing full well that Fitzroy detested him and wished him heartily away from him and from Ashton Park. Such a reaction did not trouble him, however. Over the years, Crawton had become quite hardened to people's unfavorable opinions of him. The truth was that he did not care enough for other people's opinions to be troubled by them. He glanced around the room until his eyes alit on Violet.

"Who is the very tall young woman?" he inquired curiously, nodding toward her.

Fitzroy forced himself to answer. "That is Miss Leigh," he responded, his voice wooden.

"Marianne Leigh's daughter?" Crawton's eyes widened in surprise. "One would scarcely suspect they are relatives."

Fitzroy did not answer, not wishing to discuss either lady—or anyone or anything else—with Crawton.

"I believe that I must make her acquaintance," he said, nodding at Fitzroy and strolling across the room toward Violet. "I shan't ask you to introduce me, Fitzroy, because I know doing so would offend your sense of propriety." His tone announced that he found Fitzroy's view pitifully amusing.

Outraged by Crawton's manner and by his interest in Violet, Fitzroy watched him introduce himself and join the party making the kissing boughs. Crawton leaned close to her at one point and spoke, and Fitzroy saw her recoil and stare at him in much the same manner one would regard a snake. It took considerable self-control for Fitzroy to keep from picking up the poker and rearranging Crawton's curls and cravat for him. He reminded himself that he could not make a scene in Ashton's drawing room, so he forced himself to his feet and strolled over to Violet's side.

"I beg your pardon, Miss Leigh," he said, his

voice casual. "I believe that your brother has asked for your help in the entry hall."

Violet looked up at him gratefully. She was well aware that Adrian would not have sent for her and that Fitzroy had come upon an errand of mercy, to deliver her from the decided attentions of Lord Crawton. She cast a worried glance at Fitzroy, though, and looked back toward Cynthia and Miss Langley, who would be left to the mercies of Lord Crawton if Violet departed.

"Oh, Crawton, I almost forgot," Fitzroy said, improvising hastily, "Mr. Ashton asked to see you. I believe he has gone to the library."

Crawton looked at him distrustfully, certain that he was making up the message, but good manners prohibited anything except making his bow to the ladies and departing.

Violet smiled her thanks at Fitzroy, who bowed politely and went away to confide his small success to Halliday. Mr. Randall soon reappeared in the drawing room, having done his decorating duty in the dining room with Mr. and Mrs. Haynes and Miss Thaxton. The sound of distant merriment indicated that Adrian and his companions had made their way to the billiards room. A hasty check there assured her that they were devoting themselves to decorating their hideaway, and the bust of some unknown Ashton ancestor now sported a wreath of holly hung rakishly over one ear.

"Will you be attending church tomorrow morning, Miss Leigh?" inquired Mr. Randall upon her return to the drawing room. "I understand that the Ashtons and a few of their guests will be going."

Violet nodded. "I enjoy the service on Christmas morning. I should hate to miss it."

"Then I will see you there," he said, smiling. "Perhaps you might do me the honor of riding with me?"

"I would love to," she responded warmly, glad to know that it was the truth. It was pleasant to find that she looked forward to talking with him. She had not felt so comfortable talking with a man for some time.

When she went up to bed that evening, she carried a basket of holly, ivy, and ribbons, ready to decorate the mantel in her chamber so that all was ready for the twelve days of Christmas to begin.

CHAPTER 12

As Christmas Eve melted into Christmas Day, Percival Fitzroy retired to bed with very mixed feelings. He was pleased not to be in Crawton's company, but decidedly uncomfortable on the cot in Halliday's chamber and irritated that he had been forced to relinquish his own chamber. He was pleased with himself for interfering with Crawton's unwanted attentions to Miss Leigh, but unsettled that she should have to contend with those attentions in the first place. He was, he felt with satisfaction, for the moment free of Jocko, who would not know where to find him, but he was unhappy that he was still anywhere within Jocko's range of activity. Most of all, however, he was unhappy that Halliday was still sitting downstairs in the company of several other gentlemen, gambling once again. Fitzroy had thought his friend had gotten beyond all that during his exile in the Indies, and he was fearful that Halliday would once more lose all that he had gained.

He slept fitfully, tossing and turning so much that when he finally fell out of the cot at such an early hour, he decided it was an omen. He had not planned to attend morning services, but now suddenly felt that he should. The curtains were firmly pulled 'round Halliday's bed, so Fitzroy felt no compunction in staggering from his cot and ringing for Briggs. Halliday slept soundly, so he would never notice the activity nor the lights in his chamber as Briggs labored to prepare Fitzroy for the morning. Finally, satisfied that the crisp white folds of his neckcloth were faultlessly arranged in the fashionable Oriental, his breeches were immaculate, his waistcoat a thing of beauty with its buttons brightly polished, and his boots gleaming in the firelight, he nodded at Briggs and paused in front of the glass to tuck a sprig of holly in his lapel. One must, after all, be festive.

From the gallery overlooking the entry hall, he could see a small group waiting there for the carriages to be brought 'round from the stables. Their reaction to his unexpected appearance was most gratifying, assuring Fitzroy that he had done the proper thing in coming with Halliday on this excursion to an outpost of civilization rather than accepting one of his several invitations for the holidays to far more fashionable homes.

He did not ever go to his own home. Fitzroy and his father did not quarrel, but they took no joy in one another's company, so Fitzroy seldom encountered him and never spent the holidays with him, choosing instead the company of friends. Coming with Halliday to Ashton Park had been a considerable sacrifice, but one that he felt he must make for the sake of his oldest and best friend. As he strolled down the stairway and saw the admiration in the upturned faces, he realized that his decision offered other compensations.

"Why, Mr. Fitzroy!" exclaimed Miss Thaxton, her

eyes bright, "We had not the slightest notion that you planned to join us this morning! What a very pleasant surprise!"

Her welcome was echoed by Mr. and Mrs. Ashton, Mr. and Mrs. Haynes, and Miss Leigh, as well as another lady whose name he had not yet committed to memory. He saw that Arthur Randall was the only other single gentleman present.

"How delightful that you have arisen in time to join us," said Mrs. Ashton, clearly impressed both by her guest's effort and by his magnificence. "Everyone else is still asleep and I daresay will still be so when we return."

As the vehicles rolled up the gravel sweep, she ushered him out to their carriage, saying, "There is just enough room for all of us in our chaise, and Mr. Randall is to drive Miss Leigh."

Fitzroy pondered this tidbit of information with interest, for he quite liked Miss Leigh, despite her close association with the dreaded Jocko. He felt that Halliday had treated her shabbily, and it had pleased him no end when she had flatly turned down his friend's proposal. It was very likely the healthiest thing that had ever happened to Halliday, in fact. He had never taken anything or anyone seriously, and he had always been sublimely confident of his own ability to extricate himself from any situation. Having a young woman reject him—particularly a young woman whom he assumed would be grateful for his attentions—had been a rude awakening, as had the realization that he must now decide what to do about his estates. His father might have created the problem for him, but it had been left to him to resolve it.

Fitzroy had been impressed that Halliday had decided after his experience with Miss Leigh not to rely upon marriage as the solution. They both knew very well that he could have proposed to virtually any young lady of the *ton* and been accepted, but he had decided to attempt another route. Fitzroy, who was, as he described it, "very plump in the pocket," had not hesitated to lend his friend enough money to allow Halliday to extend his father's loan from the moneylender for another two years.

Miss Leigh's rejection had decided matters. Halliday took ship for the West Indies to inspect some property there that his father had long ago abandoned, saying that it would never again provide an income. Sugar cane was still a valuable commodity, however, and Halliday had been considering the wisdom of such a trip for some time, hoping that the two plantations that his family owned there might still be saved if they were given the proper supervision.

He labored in the West Indies for a year and a half, finally managing a lucrative harvest and selling the property at a reasonable price, for the plantations had been set to rights and could command a buyer's interest. He was able to repay his loan to Fitzroy, but he had not made enough to be able to settle the loan with the moneylender. In a very few months the time would be up once again.

Fitzroy was uneasily aware that Halliday's visit to Ashton Park had a definite purpose—Delight Ashton. Halliday had made a valiant effort and successfully delayed the loss of his family's holdings here in England, but he was left with only two methods of solving his problem: marriage or gambling.

Fitzroy could not decide which was the greater of the two evils, but he was inclined to believe it was Delight. He tried to find someone else to speak with whenever he found himself in a group with her, and he found it decidedly odd that Halliday should be considering marriage with her, of all people. Still, he knew that the chance encounter with Ashton at White's and their conversation had caused Halliday to make this journey. Marriage would indeed be the practical solution to his problem, but Fitzroy felt that he could have chosen someone that would wear upon the nerves a little less. One should, he felt, consider one's friends when marrying.

He was pleased to see that Miss Leigh appeared to have made a conquest in Arthur Randall, who was a pleasant enough young man with a comfortable estate in Devonshire. Theirs would undoubtedly be one of those amicable marriages that made them the envy of their circle, for both were notably good-tempered and intelligent.

The drive to and from the church was a most attractive one, and the service itself was comforting because of the familiarity of its ritual. The words of the King James rolled over Fitzroy like music, and the Book of Common Prayer returned him to the days when he was a boy. Passing the snug cottages put him in mind of his own home, and he began to think that he might be able to be happy there, even though it was buried in the country. He could almost visualize himself as a country squire. By the time they returned to Ashton Park, Fitzroy felt uplifted and at peace with his fellow man. He had, for the moment at least, forgotten Crawton and Jocko.

Some of the others had arisen and were having their breakfast as the churchgoers made their entry, brisk and virtuous from their outing. Halliday, Fitzroy saw at once, was not among them—but then, he had not expected it. It was very likely that he had gone to bed at about the time Fitzroy had arisen.

"I do think that one of the most pleasant things about a house party is the fact that you may take your breakfast when you will, all the way up until dinner is served," remarked Miss Thaxton, who was serving her plate with pleasure.

"That is most certainly one of its advantages," agreed Fitzroy, much struck by this observation.

At a house party, one could arise as one pleased and the sideboard was kept stocked with breakfast foods so that even those straggling in midafternoon could expect to serve themselves generously. There were few pressures, and one could follow one's own inclinations and schedule.

Miss Thaxton was, Fitzroy felt, a discerning woman, for she had already commented upon the admirable sheen of his boots and the whiteness of his linen, and she had made very sensible conversation about the value of a good servant.

He smiled and seated himself next to her at the table, doubly glad that he had done so since Delight soon wandered into the room. When she saw Miss Leigh and Arthur Randall, she scowled slightly, Fitzroy noted—a most unpleasant expression, he felt, and one that she would be wise to forego.

"Where is Mr. Halliday?" Delight asked, idly fingering a piece of toast.

When no one appeared to know, she turned around crossly and marched from the room. *Quite lacking as a hostess,* Fitzroy thought. It was just as well that Mrs. Ashton had not come back downstairs in time to witness her daughter's performance.

Breakfast was a leisurely affair, and Fitzroy had retired to the library, where he was dozing over a newspaper when Halliday entered.

"I see that you are paying the price for rising at dawn, Fitz," he remarked cheerfully, walking over to stand with his back to the fire.

"And you for staying up the entire night," he retorted, waking up abruptly. "Did you lose any money, Hal?" he demanded anxiously, even though he knew his question would irritate his friend.

"No, Fitz, I did not, but I did not win any significant amount either," he replied. "You know that I am allowing you to pry like this only because you have stood my friend. Otherwise, I should be compelled to turn my back upon you."

"Yes, well, you can turn your back upon me later," responded Fitzroy, unconcerned. "Was Crawton playing?"

Halliday nodded. "He was, but he was no great winner, either."

Fitzroy was horrified. "That is neither here nor there, Hal! Very likely it is all a take-in! He breaks even or loses for a few nights, and then he moves in for the kill! Ashton must be told about him!"

"We have had this conversation before, Fitz." Halliday's voice was patient but firm. "You cannot rush in and make accusations to our host about another guest—particularly one who is apparently his relative."

"But Ashton would not wish to see any of his guests fleeced, Hal! We must do something!"

"And we are," Halliday assured him. "I will be playing with him each night, and he will not cheat while I am at table with him."

"But what about when you're *not* at the table with him?" Fitzroy demanded. "What then?"

Halliday shrugged. "You borrow too much trouble, Fitz. I think you are making Crawton out to be a villain when he is only someone who would like to be a very bad man if he could manage it."

"He is dangerous," Fitzroy insisted. "And just last night he was troubling Miss Leigh with his attentions. I had to interfere in order to give her a little peace."

"Perhaps Miss Leigh was enjoying his attentions. Had you thought of that? Did she ask you to interfere, Fitz?"

"No, but—"

"And did she thank you for saving her from the terrible Crawton?" interrupted Halliday.

"No, but she gave me a very speaking look, and I knew *precisely* what she was thinking!" Fitzroy protested.

"You put too much stock in Miss Leigh's speaking looks, Fitz. I promise you that she can mislead you with them most amazingly."

Fitzroy stopped trying to make his case. "Well, at least she will have Mr. Randall, and his presence should be enough to keep Crawton at bay," he concluded.

"What do you mean by that, Fitz?" Halliday demanded. "What has Mr. Randall to say to anything?"

"Only that he and Miss Leigh rode to church together and that he seems most attentive to her. They appear to get on very well together."

"And both of them are kind. . . ." murmured Halliday thoughtfully.

Fitzroy looked at him blankly. "What are you talking about, Hal? Naturally both of them are kind."

"Nothing at all, Fitz, nothing at all. Merely that this visit to Ashton Park is turning out to be far more amusing than I had thought it would be."

"Amusing?" demanded Fitzroy crossly. "And just what has provided the amusement, may I ask? I, for one, have seen little enough to provide amusement."

"Come now, Fitz, you are a part of it yourself."

"A part of *what*?"

"The amusing comedy of mankind," replied Halliday.

"Do you know, Hal, sometimes I think that you are touched in your upper works—or perhaps you just wish to stir me up in order to see me irritated!" His peace of mind was gone as suddenly as it had come. "And I think that we made a *serious* error in judgment in coming to Ashton Park!"

He rose and walked abruptly from the library, seriously ruffled in spirit, leaving Halliday standing in front of the fire, looking after him ruefully.

"I begin to think that you may be correct, Fitz," he said slowly, as the door closed and he was left alone in the library.

CHAPTER 13

Violet spent a gloriously idle Christmas afternoon. After reassuring herself that Adrian and Cynthia were harmlessly occupied in the billiards room with the other young people, she accepted Mr. Randall's invitation for a walk.

The day was brisk but clear, and the gentleman's manner unassuming—quite different from the most unwelcome advances made by Lord Crawton the previous evening. She had not yet seen Crawton that day, and she allowed herself to hope that she would not see him at all. If fortune smiled upon her, she decided, he would have chosen to go elsewhere for the holiday. In the meantime, however, she had her walk with Mr. Randall and she put such unpleasant thoughts as Lord Crawton firmly from her mind.

"Well, Miss Leigh," he said cheerfully as they set forth, "you know Ashton Park far better than I. Which direction should we take?"

She considered the matter for a moment. "Perhaps since we walked through some of the more remote section yesterday, you might enjoy seeing the shrubbery walk." She looked at him questioningly. "Or, there is a small stream beyond the apple orchards, with a very picturesque little bridge that leads to nowhere in particular. Or, should we feel very ambitious, there is a charming village that is about an hour's walk from here."

He smiled at her. "There will be an early dinner today; perhaps we should limit ourselves to the shrubbery walk."

Violet nodded, well satisfied with his choice, and accepted his arm as they strolled across the lawn.

"Mrs. Ashton takes great pride in her puzzle garden," she observed. "She told us that it took her some four years to get it finally just to her liking."

"And do you enjoy such planning?" Mr. Randall inquired. He had to look up at her just a little, for he was slightly shorter than she, but he did not seem to mind. "Are you interested in gardens, too?"

"It would be better to say that I enjoy them," she replied. "I very much like to walk in them and to admire whatever shrubs or plants are in season, but I have no skills in managing formal gardens. Now a kitchen garden," she added, "that is quite a different matter. I am able to cultivate herbs and vegetables. We have quite an extensive kitchen garden at Richland, and when we are home, I take great pleasure working in it."

He looked at her with interest. "So you enjoy a quiet life in the country, Miss Leigh? You are not like some that must always be in London or traveling from one great house to another for a series of visits and parties?"

She shook her head. "I would not enjoy such a rootless life at all. I love Richland and our life there." She paused a moment, then smiled a little ruefully. "The rest of my family greatly prefers a less rural life, however, so I go wherever they wish to go."

"You and I are much in accord," he told her, as they entered the maze of shrubbery and started down one of its paths. "Perhaps you and your family could visit me in Kent. Since my uncle's death, I have not been there often, and it is time that I set it to rights. I should enjoy showing it to you, and having you advise me upon the serious matter of the kitchen garden."

"How charming," observed Delight, as Violet and Mr. Randall made a sharp turn in the maze and came face-to-face with her and Mr. Halliday. "I think that kitchen gardens are precisely the kind of thing that Violet should give her time to."

Violet smiled at Mr. Randall, who looked taken aback by both Delight's remark and her tone. "You must not mind Miss Ashton," she informed him kindly. "She very frequently suffers from dyspepsia, and we must be understanding when she is a trifle shrewish."

Turning her smile upon Delight, who was eyeing her angrily, she added, "I would recommend a cup of chamomile tea, Delight. It will do wonders for you."

And so saying, she and Mr. Randall moved past the other two and continued into the maze.

Christmas dinner was a jolly affair, and the number of guests was increased by neighbors who had come just for dinner and the dancing afterwards. There were pheasant pies and steak pies, roast goose and a great chine of beef, countless side dishes, mince pies, and plum pudding. The Ashtons were generous hosts, and the number of their guests rapidly outgrew the number that could be seated at the dining table. Small tables were quickly set up in every space available in the dining room, and the servants had to maneuver their way through the maze with the greatest of care. No one seemed to mind, however, and many toasts were drunk that evening.

Violet was enjoying it all much more than she had expected, and she knew that a good part of the reason was the company of Arthur Randall. She had spent the better part of the day with him, and they, along with Mr. Fitzroy and Miss Thaxton, were seated at one of the smaller tables at dinner. They were very merry, and after dinner the company made their way into the drawing room and adjacent morning room, which had been emptied of furniture to accommodate dancing, and the doors opened wide into the twin drawing room beyond them, which had also been cleared. Card tables had been set up in the library, and one of the older ladies had seated herself at the pianoforte in the drawing room and begun to play.

Adrian and Cynthia and the other young people had been seated at the foot of the dining table together, and as the music began, they hurried in to take their places for the first dance. Violet had noticed that Cynthia seemed to be practicing her flirtatious wiles on all of the young gentlemen impartially, and she was comforted to see that at least she had picked no particular flirt. Violet could be only grateful for that, although it seemed to her that perhaps her sister might be behaving a trifle wilder than she should. Still, it was Christmas, and all of them were high-spirited, including her mother, who was preparing to stand up with Mr. Chesterton. So long as Cynthia did nothing especially outrageous, Violet felt that they could make the best of the situation. Indeed, she could not keep from laughing as she watched the younger ones practicing their bows and curtseys as the dancers assembled.

Mrs. Ashton gave pride of place to her daughter, and had Delight and her partner open the ball with the first dance. Her partner, naturally enough, was Mr. Halliday. Together they led the other couples out in a minuet, and the youngsters had great need of their polished curtseys and bows. Violet was aware that Delight was trying to catch her eye—triumphantly, no doubt—and she studiously avoided eye contact with that lady. Nonetheless, she enjoyed her dance with Mr. Randall, and they stood up together for the quadrille.

To her displeasure, Lord Crawton bore down upon her at the close of that dance and, not wishing to be unmannerly when she was a guest in the Ashton home and he an Ashton relative, she reluctantly stood up with him for the next dance. She saw that Delight was once more partnered with Mr. Halliday, but she had no time for other observations, for she was fully occupied in holding Lord Crawton at bay. Whenever they came close to one another during the figures of the dance, he came far too close, and he was given to trying to whisper to her. All of her composure was necessary to keep herself from shuddering upon such occasions, but she carefully maintained a frosty distance.

When the dance was over, he bowed to her and

thanked her, saying, "You are quite as cool as the weather, Miss Leigh—but then, that makes you all the more enticing, as I am certain you know."

Violet dropped him a brief curtsey, avoiding both a reply and the gentleman's eye, turning quite blindly to the gentleman standing next to her.

"I believe that this is our dance, Miss Leigh," she heard a familiar voice say, and she realized that Mr. Halliday was the one standing next to her.

Grateful to be saved from another dance with Crawton, even given the challenge of Mr. Halliday's company, she allowed him to lead her onto the floor once more. Once again, she was grateful that the figures of the dance prohibited any sustained conversation, and once again, she resolutely avoided the gentleman's eye.

"Did you enjoy your walk in the garden today, Miss Leigh?" Halliday inquired blandly, as the dance brought them close.

"Naturally," she returned. "And did you, sir?"

"But of course," he responded, sounding amused. "I could scarcely say otherwise, could I, without being wretchedly wanting in manners?"

"I had no notion that you troubled yourself about such things." She smiled gently, although still without eye contact, and was grateful that she had the opportunity to link arms with another gentleman and leave her own partner behind.

When she rejoined him once more, he looked at her reproachfully. "I am desolate that you should think me mannerless, ma'am. How could I prove to you that I am not?"

She shook her head lightly. "You have nothing to prove to me, Mr. Halliday," she assured him. "Make yourself easy upon that count. If you wish for me to think you mannerly, why, naturally, I shall do so."

He grinned at her, looking her directly in the eye, reminding her sharply of how few men were able to do so and of the warmth of his gaze. "That does not sound at all like you, Miss Leigh. You will consent to think me mannerly simply because I wish you to do so?"

"You sound surprised, sir. Do you think me so disagreeable, then?"

"Not at all, Miss Leigh," he said, his tone sincere, "but certainly most deplorably honest. They are, I find, occasionally the same thing."

Violet was forced to laugh. "You make me sound quite odious, sir."

"Then I have done what I would never wish to do," he replied, his voice and his gaze both softening, "for you could never be so."

Taken by surprise, she glanced at him, and was caught off balance by a glimpse of tenderness, a reminder of what she had seen in him when they first met.

"Then it is clear, Mr. Halliday, that you do not know me well. You have only to ask my brother or sister to know the truth of the matter."

Fortunately for her peace of mind, they soon came to the end of the dance, and she was able to retire to the safety of being a lady checking upon the welfare of others. Adrian and Cynthia received her immediate attention, and Mrs. Leigh soon thereafter. Standing to one side, Halliday watched with amusement—and some sympathy—her attempt to shepherd her flock. Adrian evaded her and went away to play cards, and Cynthia followed Miss Langley upstairs to discuss the evening.

After a late supper of cold goose and *blanc mange* and jellies, cold pheasant pie and tarts and sandwiches, those guests who had come from neighboring houses departed, wishing a happy Christmas to those of Ashton Park. Those left behind entertained themselves for a while longer, the younger ones playing games and dancing, the older ones chatting and playing cards.

Violet had enjoyed herself, having danced every dance, even though the last one was with a young man approximately a head shorter than she was. She had not allowed that to take from her pleasure, however, for the youthful gentleman had been determined to do his best to be merry and she had done her best to keep pace with him.

As the last of the guests departed, Mrs. Ashton turned to her with a satisfied smile.

"Well, Violet, what did you think? Was it well done? Did everyone enjoy themselves?"

"It was a great success, ma'am," Violet assured her sincerely. "It was a splendid beginning to the twelve days of Christmas."

Mrs. Ashton's normally gray face lit up. "Yes, it was, wasn't it? Quite a good way to begin." Satisfied, she turned back to direct the maids that were bringing candles for the older guests who were ready to have their way lighted up to bed.

Violet was not ready to retire just yet, however, and she went in search of Adrian and Cynthia, who were engaged with the younger members in a game of forfeits. Violet sat and watched them for a while, then collected Cynthia and Miss Langley, announcing that it was more than time for them to go upstairs and sending them on their way.

Satisfied that her duty was done, she lingered for a while at the fire in the drawing room, thinking about Richland and wishing herself there, then turned to the entry hall, where she could collect her own candle and go upstairs.

She had thought herself alone, for the gentlemen still awake were playing cards, and most of the ladies had already gone upstairs. As Violet took her candle and started for the stairs, however, she realized that she was no longer alone. A darkness suddenly overshadowed her, and she turned to see Lord Crawton standing between her and the light of the chandelier.

Before she could speak, he clutched her tightly and she could feel his hot breath on her cheek. He pressed his lips to hers, holding her in place with a grip that she would not have thought him capable of, releasing her only when he was ready.

She longed to slap him quite across the room, but she had no wish to make a scene and she knew that gentlemen in their cups were very often guilty of indiscreet behavior. Instead of striking him, she pulled herself away and pointed to the stairs.

"If you are going upstairs, Lord Crawton, please do so."

He smiled—a particularly reptilian smile. "I believe, Miss Leigh, that I am not quite prepared for bed. Your kiss has inspired me to—how shall I say?—to go forth and make my fortune tonight."

The retort that sprang to Violet's lips was scarcely ladylike, nor was it sufficient for the occasion, so she remained silent as he turned and walked toward the library.

After he disappeared, Violet concentrated very hard on walking toward the stairs. With her candle still clutched in her hand, she turned once more toward the stairway.

To her horror, she was stopped once more.

This time, the gentleman was Mr. Halliday.

"Miss Leigh," he said, pulling her close to him, "I believe that we are under the kissing bough, so I am free to give you a kiss."

Violet looked up and saw that it was true. She was under the kissing bough. She shuddered.

"You need not recoil, ma'am. I assure you that I realize you do not care for me—but tonight I take advantage of the holiday. And I noted that Lord Crawton did the same."

Here he pulled her close and kissed her. The warmth of his closeness and the intensity of his kiss shook her so deeply that she thought her knees might give way. Indeed, if he had not held her so firmly, she was certain that they would have done so. By the time he released her, she had regained command of herself, but she could not bring herself to look at him.

Instead, turning without a word, she took her unlighted candle and fled up the stairs into the darkness above.

Gentlemen, it appeared, were all the same, and she tried not to think about it as she prepared for bed that night. Try as she would, however, she could not forget Mr. Halliday's nearness and the answering wave of warmth that had swept over her, threatening to make her forget who she was and what she expected of herself. *How much pleasure it would give him to know my reaction,* she thought bitterly! *How satisfying for him to know that the lady who had rejected his offer had longed for his embrace*! But he would, she promised herself, *never* know.

Sleep was long in coming that night.

CHAPTER 14

Violet awakened as unsettled as she had been when she went to sleep. The thought of Lord Crawton's advances made her flesh crawl, but Mr. Halliday's unexpected performance under the kissing bough had upset her even more. She was certain that she could manage Crawton well enough, but she was not at all certain that she could manage her feelings about Mr. Halliday so successfully.

It was most unfortunate that he had come to Ashton Park for the holidays. Even though she fully expected him to make an offer for Delight, Mr. Halliday's presence caused her to think about him far more than she wished to. She knew that she could not—and would not—wish that she had accepted his offer herself. The very fact that he would offer for Delight proved to her that everything that she had thought about him had been correct. Still, seeing him every day—and in such a setting where contact could not be avoided—was distressing. Her reaction to his kiss last night had overset her completely. Just why he had decided to force himself upon her in such a manner mystified her, but she was determined to think about it as little as possible.

Accordingly, she did not think about him for the next quarter hour, until she went down to breakfast. She found Mr. Halliday there, as she expected, along with Mrs. Ashton, Mr. Randall, Mr. Fitzroy, and a few other guests. What shocked her was to see her brother there, also.

"Adrian! Whatever has gotten you up at such an early hour?" she demanded, smiling at him. "I thought that you were planning to sit up late last night."

"And so I did, Vi," he assured her. "I sat up the entire night," he added in satisfaction.

Violet's heart sank. She was certain that he had been gambling. "Indeed?" she responded, keeping her tone light. It would not do to even hint at her displeasure when they were in company.

He nodded, attempting to look nonchalant, but gave up the pretense almost immediately. "I had an amazing evening, Vi! I don't wish to brag, but I did very well indeed!"

Mr. Halliday nodded. "I can attest to that, Miss Leigh. He would have cleaned my pockets completely if I had remained in the game."

Adrian flushed with pleasure at this remark. "I'm not such a nodcock as to think that," he replied. "If you had played another hand, I daresay you would have won it back from me."

Violet saw that her brother's initial fondness for Mr. Halliday had not lessened. If anything, it had grown into full-blown hero worship. She remembered, with a sudden dip of her heart, what Lord

Crawton had said after accosting her: that he was going in to try to make his fortune at cards.

"Who else was playing with you two?" she inquired, hoping that her tone was suitably casual. "Were you with them, Mr. Fitzroy?"

He shook his head. "I went to bed after the dancing was over with, I'm afraid. Halliday has been accusing me of getting old."

"Surely not, sir," she responded. She smiled politely and waited to see if she would learn anything else.

"Lamb and Delaney played, of course," contributed Adrian. "And Mr. Agnew as well."

"After Fitz abandoned us, our host joined us, too—as did Lord Crawton," added Mr. Halliday. "But Mr. Leigh came away the winner."

Fitzroy's fork fell from his hand and crashed to his plate, but he picked it up hurriedly and resumed his breakfast, casting a sidelong glance at Halliday.

"Well," said Violet brightly, "after such a long night, Adrian, you will assuredly want to get a full night's rest tonight."

Her brother looked at her in disbelief. "With a run of luck like this, Vi?" he demanded. "I shall go to bed shortly and get up in the afternoon. That will be more than enough rest for me."

She could see that she was making no headway, so she abandoned the subject and turned the conversation to plans for the day's activities.

Mr. Fitzroy declared himself ready for an invigorating walk—so long as it took him no more than half an hour, whereupon he would retire to the library and the most recent newspaper. Mrs.

Ashton placidly announced her intention to take a stroll through her gardens after conferring with her cook, and Mr. Randall said, glancing at Violet, that he had hoped to walk to the village, having heard that it was quite an attractive place. Violet smiled at him and declared herself ready to undertake such an adventure. As she went up to change into sturdy walking boots and a warm pelisse, her brother and his friends adjourned to sleep the first part of the day away. At least, thought Violet, she could enjoy her walk without worrying about Adrian. If her luck held, her mother and Cynthia would sleep until early afternoon.

When at last Violet and Mr. Randall set off for their walk, their group had grown to include Mr. and Mrs. Haynes, Mr. Agnew, Miss Langley—and Delight and Mr. Halliday. While it was not as pleasant as a walk with only Mr. Randall, Violet had to admit to herself that going alone with him on such a lengthy walk was not, perhaps, what she should have done. If she was going to preach propriety to the rest of her family, she would have to practice it herself.

Fortunately, having so many along on the walk protected her from having to be too much with Delight or Mr. Halliday. Delight seemed to be quite particular about keeping that gentleman to herself, so Violet was able to enjoy the excursion without the fear of having Mr. Halliday suddenly single her out.

In the village, they stopped for cider at the local inn and recruited their strength for the walk back, and some three hours after their departure, they were once more at Ashton Park, settling themselves for a peaceful afternoon. It was not long, however, before Violet was set upon once more.

"Come along, Vi! Come and play billiards with us!" pleaded Adrian, who had come in to remove her from the drawing room where she was talking with Mr. Randall and the Hayneses. "Or, better still, if you will all come, we'll have a game of Hunt the Slipper!"

"Hunt the Slipper!" Mrs. Haynes turned and smiled at her husband. "We always enjoy playing that, my dear. Let's join them."

Violet went willingly enough. She was fond of games and she was glad to see that Adrian and Cynthia were enjoying themselves—as long as they were not allowing things to get out of hand. She saw with amusement—and a little apprehension—that Jocko had joined them in the billiards room. Adrian had left him in Cynthia's care while he was gone, but as soon as Adrian came back into the room, Jocko hopped to his shoulder once more and prepared to play. He was, apparently, deeply interested in billiards.

After a slight rearrangement of the tables, they had enough room to form a good-sized circle for their game, and Cynthia was selected to be the first hunter.

"Come along, Cyn. Give me your slipper. We'll use yours for the whole of the game," said her brother briskly.

Cynthia relinquished one small leather slipper willingly enough, and Violet was grateful that she had not been asked for one of hers, which, decidedly larger, would have been much easier to see being passed 'round the circle.

Cynthia stood in the center, obediently covering her eyes until the count of ten while her slipper was passed from one player to another, all the while hidden behind their backs. When she opened her eyes, they were all to act as though they were still passing it while she tried to guess who actually had it.

As she counted to ten, they passed the slipper hurriedly from one to another, trying to swing close enough to one another that they would be able to pass it without being seen. When Cynthia finished counting, she opened her eyes wide and turned slowly, eyeing all of them carefully as they continued to pass the slipper or to pretend to do so. Violet was enjoying the game much more than usual, for Mr. Randall was on her right. It seemed that Hunt the Slipper had possibilities she had overlooked when she had no particular interest in those standing on either side of her.

After guessing three times, Cynthia had still failed to locate her slipper, so she had to close her eyes and count once more, while the slipper changed its home. Adrian motioned silently to his friend Delaney, who was directly across the circle from him, and then lightly tossed the slipper to him, creating a rustle of movement on each side. When Cynthia opened her eyes this time, she was keener-eyed and quicker in calling the name, and she caught Violet with the slipper still in her hand.

"So, Vi! Your turn now! Cover those eyes and count to ten!" This time Delaney motioned to Nathan Lamb, who prepared to catch the slipper.

It was not, however, Mr. Lamb who caught it. Jocko had been following the game intently and now, apparently feeling that he had mastered its rules, decided to play. Except that he did not wish to pass the slipper on. He caught it and ran from the room, chattering loudly.

"Great Jupiter! Jocko, come back here with Cynthia's shoe!" shouted Adrian, sprinting after his pet.

Violet's eyes flew open and she, too, started after Jocko. All too soon, everyone from the game was in pursuit, while Jocko, now the heart and soul of the game, did his part by running ahead of them as quickly as he could. When he reached the stairway, he scampered up the railing, rearranging the holly and ivy as he went. Several footmen had entered into the chase, and people were coming from other parts of the house to see what all the noise was about.

Halliday, who had been in the library playing cards with several of the other gentlemen, came to the door just in time to see Jocko fly up the stairs. It was Crawton who appeared on the gallery just as Jocko reached it. Seeing the slipper clutched in the monkey's paw and the pack of shrieking youngsters behind him, Crawton reached out and grabbed Jocko. Jocko naturally took exception to this violent treatment of his person, and immediately nipped Crawton's hand.

The ensuing scene was not a pretty one. Crawton flung the little monkey to the floor and clutched his hand, cursing. Cynthia shrieked because Jocko had been mistreated, Jocko shrieked for the same reason, Adrian yelled for Delaney and Lamb to keep an eye peeled in case Jocko made a fresh break for freedom. Mrs. Ashton, who had gained the entry hall in time to see that Lord Crawton had been victimized, instructed the butler to bring him some smelling salts and a glass of brandy.

"It would be as well to wash that wound, ma'am," Halliday told her, "although I daresay just pouring a little brandy over it would do the trick."

As Crawton started back to his room, clutching his hand and cursing, Fitzroy watched him go. "Do you know, Hal," he said in wonder, "I almost begin to feel an affection for the little beast."

Halliday nodded, but he was watching Violet as she turned to speak quietly with Arthur Randall. In a moment, though, she turned and moved back toward the stairs alone.

Curious now, Halliday followed her quietly and looked around the corner when she started down one of the wings of bedrooms. She spoke to a maid who was bringing a tray with the brandy and took it from her, walking into what had formerly been Fitzroy's chamber.

The door had been left ajar and Halliday moved quietly to it, peering through the crack.

"Just see what that damnable beast has done to me!" he exclaimed, holding out his hand for her to inspect.

"I daresay he did not like being grabbed, Lord Crawton," she responded pleasantly. "Most of us do not, you know."

"Certainly you are not going to bring up last night at a time like this, Miss Leigh!" he protested.

"I think it is an excellent time, particularly since Jocko and I seem to have so much in common. We neither of us like having someone lay hands upon us by force."

Crawton muttered something that Halliday could not understand, and then Violet snapped, "Oh, do stop making a fuss over something that is no more than a scratch, sir!" She looked at him for a moment then added slowly, "Or at least it will probably come to nothing."

"What do you mean by that? First you say it is a scratch, and then you look as though it could be something more! For God's sake, Miss Leigh, what are you talking about?"

"Well," she said, measuring her words, "sometimes even a tiny scratch can be fatal, I'm afraid."

Lord Crawton, normally quite swarthy, blanched. "Fatal?" he croaked. "Why? What happens?"

Violet shrugged. "No one knows. After all, monkeys like Jocko come from faraway lands, and we don't know just why some people die after receiving only the lightest of bites."

"How long does it take?" he asked, his eyes glued to her face.

She shook her head. "I have read that it varies. For some, it has been as long as two weeks, but one poor man collapsed the very night he was bitten."

"What can I do, Miss Leigh?" he asked, his voice growing feeble.

"I would suggest that you get as much rest as possible and that you keep the wound very clean," she replied, her mind working busily.

She had placed a washbasin before him so that he could wash his hand, which he did very carefully, and she then poured some of the brandy across the wound while she appeared to think the matter over.

"Now, if you drink the rest of that, I imagine that you should feel very much more the thing, Lord Crawton," she said briskly.

"Damned animal ought to be shot!" he muttered.

"Nonsense!" she replied sharply. "You simply need to keep your hands off him, sir. And hurting Jocko would make you look exceedingly foolish. I can imagine what people would say about your quarreling with a monkey."

Having planted him a facer and leveled him, Violet turned toward the door, happy to be going. Halliday, chuckling at what he had seen and overheard, hurried on around the corner, but not before he heard her parting shot at the door.

"I think that you should avoid touching anything with that hand, Lord Crawton." Her tone was earnest. "I would suggest that you not dance or play cards or do anything that would cause you to touch your hand to anyone or anything. If you do that, and if you rest a very great deal in your room, that rest might help you make it through the next two weeks. And, once you have survived that period of time, you might very well expect to live a normal life."

Crawton's face had paled even more at the mention of surviving the next two weeks, and he nodded feverishly.

"Yes, I shall do so!" he said. "Rest assured that I shall do so, Miss Leigh!"

Satisfied with her handiwork, the details of which had been made up on the spot, Violet left his chamber, closing the door firmly behind her and smiling.

Jocko, she thought, was quite an excellent little animal and she determined to give him an extra treat with his dinner.

CHAPTER 15

For the next few days, Lord Crawton kept to his room, and Violet enjoyed her reprieve. Even though she knew Adrian was still playing cards into the early morning, she was not so troubled now that she knew Lord Crawton was not among those playing. She had been long enough in London to have heard a few of the rumors about his methods of gambling and to worry about what he might entice a youngster like Adrian to do. And, while she knew that Mr. Halliday was a gamester, she did not fear him as she did Crawton. Just why this was, she did not trouble to ask herself.

Mr. Randall remained very attentive and, although she enjoyed his attentions and found it pleasant to know that someone was eager for her company, she noticed that when he took her arm, she felt very calm. It was a comforting gesture and she was aware of a fondness for the gentleman, but her heart did not hammer as it did when Mr. Halliday was close to her. The difference in feeling confirmed her opinion that her peace of mind would best be kept by a marriage to someone like Mr. Randall—should she marry at all.

The days since Jocko's participation in Hunt the

Slipper had been pleasant and peaceful. He had not broken loose again to visit his fellow players, much to the relief of both Violet and Mr. Fitzroy. Despite the fact that he felt more kindly toward the monkey since his attack on Crawton, Fitzroy did not look forward to any close personal contact.

The guests had whiled away their time by riding, playing games, reading and taking long walks, and dancing after dinner with Violet at the pianoforte. She was grateful to be safely ensconced behind the instrument, having no obligation to participate in the dancing. Mrs. Haynes had offered to take her place, but Violet had told her cheerfully that she was enjoying herself; Mrs. Haynes could return to her dancing with a clear conscience.

Adrian had taken his new curricle out every day. Violet knew that Mr. Halliday had consented to ride with him once, and had even given him some advice on holding the ribbons. "For he's a member of the Four-in-Hand, Vi, and you must know that he's considered a top-sawyer!" he had told her eagerly. Adrian longed for nothing so much as the right to wear the bright yellow-striped waistcoat of that exclusive club.

She had merely smiled, grateful that his interest had moved in another direction from gambling, though it seemed to her that he had just exchanged one evil for another. Now she must hope that he would not break his neck by oversetting the curricle as he tried to take a corner at too great a rate of speed.

"Halliday told me that I must hold down my speed until I can master the turns," he added in discontent. "He said that I would look no how if I landed my curricle in a ditch and had to be towed out by a farm cart."

"Well, that is a very practical point to consider," Violet had agreed, "and Mr. Halliday would certainly know about such matters."

Violet was surprised by such a stricture from Mr. Halliday but very grateful for it. Adrian would listen to him on such a matter while he would pay no heed to a sister who knew nothing of driving.

She was aware that Adrian and Cynthia and the other young people had been whispering among themselves, and she had no doubt that they were conspiring, but she did not know to what end. Periodically they had disappeared for an hour or so at a time, and she had noticed ink stains on her sister's fingers—and Cynthia was not fond of letter writing, so Violet knew that something else was afoot. Finally, however, they explained their doings when everyone had gathered in the drawing room after dinner. Cynthia and Miss Langley, flushed with excitement, pushed Adrian forward to present their idea.

Adrian cleared his throat importantly and puffed out his chest a little. "It occurred to us," he began, gesturing toward the gaggle of youngsters gathered around him, "that while we are all together for such a lengthy space of time, we should have a project to occupy ourselves."

A spattering of applause and encouragement broke forth from the gaggle, whose number had swelled with the recent arrival of Adrian's friends Freddie and Beaver, who had made good their threat to drop in unannounced. Mrs. Ashton had received them placidly, always grateful for the addition of eligible young men.

"Hear, hear!" called Beaver.

"Just what sort of project do you have in mind?" inquired Mr. Halliday, watching them with amusement.

Adrian cleared his throat portentously and the others watched him anxiously. "We thought it should be something that everyone could take part in," he explained, "and what could be better than"—here he paused for dramatic effect and looked around the room, pleased to see that he had everyone's attention—"a play!"

The gaggle immediately broke into wild applause and cheering.

"A theatrical!" exclaimed Mrs. Ashton, with an unusual show of enthusiasm. "Why, that would be the very thing!"

"What play will you give?" asked Violet. "Something by Shakespeare?"

The gaggle stared at her in disbelief, then broke into a fit of merriment.

"Of course not," replied Adrian hurriedly, attempting to cover his sister's gaffe. "We have chosen something much more up-to-date: *The Lover's Vengeance.*"

"Really?" responded Violet weakly, searching her memory for such a play.

"Yes, it is a splendid play because it isn't *just* about lovers, you see. It has a murder and a villainous uncle who tries to keep his niece from marrying and taking away her fortune from his care, and there are two other pairs of lovers and a large group of people at a party and a mix-up of identities! There is, in short, something for everyone!" he said proudly.

"Yes, and everyone can have a part—or at least help with the play by prompting the actors!" added Cynthia. "Diana and I have copied out all the parts."

"And I suppose that you have cast the parts already?" inquired Violet, certain of the answer.

Adrian attempted to look modest. "Well, we did give the matter a great deal of thought during the past day or two, and I think we have worked things out pretty well."

"And who plays the niece?" demanded Delight, who had not taken part in any of the planning. She had spent little time with the rest of the young people, having chosen to remain as close to Mr. Halliday as she possibly could.

Adrian, who was nobody's fool, had foreseen her interest in the leading role. Having dealt with Delight all his life, he was well aware that, if she were discontent, the project would be scotched immediately.

"Well, we thought that you would be good for the role," he began reluctantly, "but if you don't care to do it, we can recast it, of course."

Delight smiled smugly, glancing swiftly at Violet. "Of course I shall do it," she assured him. "I am very fond of plays, and I shall do the part justice."

Adrian nodded in satisfaction and there was a rustle of approval from the gaggle, who also recognized the danger posed by Delight.

"And what of Mr. Halliday?" she asked. "What is his part?"

The gaggle stiffened apprehensively.

Adrian grinned at Mr. Halliday. "We thought that *you,* sir, should have the honor of playing the uncle."

Delight gasped and Halliday looked startled. Violet was forced to feign a fit of coughing so that she could retire behind her handkerchief while she regained her composure. Mr. Halliday had clearly not thought of himself in terms of a villainous uncle.

"It's quite those best part, sir," Adrian explained enthusiastically. "We must have someone who is tall and imposing and who could strike the fear of God into everyone else."

Halliday looked even more taken aback by this tribute. He had certainly never seen himself in such a light, and he was not all certain that he was flattered.

"Well, *I* don't think he should play such a role!" announced Delight petulantly. "Who is to play opposite me?"

"Freddie," he answered promptly, ignoring his friend's smothered sigh. Freddie Tilton was known for his excellent sense of fashion and his equally excellent address. He had been chosen as the sacrificial lamb to Delight's vanity. "He has quite the best voice among us, and we thought that he would be an excellent foil for you."

Delight's face cleared. "We will, after all, play most of our scenes together," she said, turning to Mr. Halliday as though to comfort him. "I have seen this play, and we shall be able to do it excellently."

Violet was deeply amused, both by Adrian's adept handling of Delight and by Mr. Halliday's discomfiture at the casting. She was quite certain that he had never pictured himself as either a villain or as the uncle of a young woman Delight's age. While Mr. Chesterton or Mr. Ashton might have played the part more nearly for age, she had to admit that Adrian was correct about Mr. Halliday being the only one of them capable of striking fear into the hearts of those assembled.

Once the hurdle of casting Delight and Mr. Halliday had been cleared, the gaggle fell to work. By afternoon they had assembled a rehearsal area, assigned all the parts, and begun practicing them. Violet was surprised to learn that she was one of the lovers and that Mr. Randall had been paired with her. She discerned Adrian's fine hand behind this, but she accepted it gracefully. Adrian had taken on the management of the play, and he was taking his responsibility seriously.

Mr. Fitzroy was somewhat unsettled to find that he had been cast as butler to the villainous uncle. He looked very doubtful about this, but Adrian hurried to reassure him.

"You are the only one of us with the proper dignity to be a butler, Mr. Fitzroy," he explained. Then he added, grinning, "And you are also the one that gets to stab the villainous uncle at the end of the play!"

Fitzroy glanced at Halliday. "Well, I must admit that there is some comfort in that," he admitted. "Must I wait until the end?"

"You'll do famously," replied Adrian, "and you shall enjoy it hugely. We all shall!"

The older ones found themselves carried forward on a tidal wave of youthful enthusiasm, and their hours became consumed with learning parts, assembling costumes and sets, and—finally—beginning actual rehearsals.

"We can't present the play on Twelfth Night, for Mrs. Ashton has planned a masquerade ball, so we should give it two nights before that," Adrian announced. "That will give us time to be properly prepared, and we will have a day to recover from our efforts."

"Who will our audience be?" inquired Miss Langley, a lively, good-humored young lady who was enjoying the undertaking immensely. "We must have an audience other than ourselves."

"Naturally we will," Delight assured her. She would have done nothing without an audience. "I shall have my mother invite all the neighbors, and we shall follow our performance with an excellent supper!"

Satisfied that they would have someone to appreciate their efforts, Miss Langley and the others returned to their work with renewed enthusiasm. Mr. Fitzroy learned his lines in the first afternoon and insisted upon rehearsing the stabbing scene with Halliday.

"I just want to get it firmly in my mind, Hal," he explained. "We should, perhaps, repeat it several times so that I can remember just how it goes." He moved toward his friend once more, lifting the collapsible stage knife above him in a most ominous manner.

"I think once will be sufficient for the moment, Fitz," Halliday informed him dryly, removing the knife from his hand. "You have become appallingly enthusiastic. And rest assured I shall check to be certain that you do not have a *real* knife when we run through this scene again."

Violet and Mr. Randall had also practiced their lines together, and she was pleased to see that the only thing that would cause her discomfort was a scene in which he embraced her. Still, it was very mild, and she knew that he would be very circumspect.

She had been worried about Cynthia's part, but, to Violet's surprise, Adrian had kept her from having any role in which she would have a questionable line or action. To her chagrin, she had been relegated to the part of a maid. When she had complained to him that she was supposed to have one of the leading roles, Adrian had asserted his role as older brother and told her quietly that the other parts were not suitable for her or her Miss Langley. Neither of them was to be allowed to say or do anything that could be considered even mildly improper.

Violet, who witnessed all of this, was astonished by this new maturity in her brother. When she had the opportunity to inquire into the matter the next day, she seized it.

"I was very impressed to see that you were so careful of Cynthia and Miss Langley, Adrian," she told him. "Keeping them from exposing themselves to criticism was a very wise thing for you to do."

Adrian flushed. "Well, Vi, I didn't think of that at first. I should have, I admit, but we were so caught up in the excitement that I simply didn't give it a thought."

"But I heard you, Adrian. Even though she was upset, you were firm and told her she must play the maid."

Adrian shifted uncomfortably. "That was because Mr. Halliday talked it over with me," he explained. "When I was telling him all about his part as uncle—just after he found about it, you know—he asked me about Cyn and Miss Langley. That's when it came to me that I must be a little more careful about them. I forget, you know, that Cyn is still just a girl."

"You handled it very well," she told him, smiling. "And I am certain that the play will be a great success."

"Well, it will at least be great fun," he replied, his eyes brightening. "We needed something to make us a little more lively."

Excusing himself to his sister, he hurried back to the others, eager to get on with it. Violet was left to consider what he had told her. She would not have thought Mr. Halliday prone to consider the reputations of careless young girls. It was possible, she conceded to herself, that the past two years had wrought some changes in him.

CHAPTER 16

"Why, Basil! Are you feeling better?" asked Mrs. Ashton, her face wrinkled in concern.

Most of the guests had already assembled in the drawing room before dinner when Lord Crawton entered. Violet saw that he was wearing a bandage that was substantially larger than he needed.

"Somewhat better, thank you, Deirdre," he replied crossly. "Although I would not have been compelled to keep to my room if you did not house wild animals here at Ashton Park." He looked about him as though expecting Jocko to appear at any moment and set upon him.

"Come now, Basil," responded Mrs. Ashton, coaxingly. "You make that little monkey sound like a tiger. I *am* glad that you finally felt equal to joining us once more."

"I must apologize for Jocko's behavior, Lord Crawton," said Mrs. Leigh in her most charming voice, forcing herself to smile even though she disliked the man heartily. "We did not intend to bring him with us, of course, and Deirdre has been most kind about having him here."

"She can damned well afford to be kind!" he retorted. "It wasn't her hand that he ripped apart!"

Mrs. Leigh did not attempt further conversation upon the subject, and the other guests hurriedly began speaking of other things. Violet put a warning hand on her brother's arm, for he was about to say something to Crawton about addressing his mother in such a manner.

"It will not help things," she murmured. "You will merely embarrass our mother further."

Knowing she was correct, he gave it up and turned to Freddie Tilton to discuss the play.

"That monkey is a nasty little brute," said Delight to Mr. Halliday and Mr. Fitzroy. "I cannot blame my father's cousin for disliking him so." She shook her head sympathetically.

Fitzroy was torn between his dislike of Crawton and his dislike of Jocko but, upon brief reflection, Jocko won. "I don't know," he said casually. "It seems to me that he is harmless enough."

Halliday looked at him with raised brows, but Fitzroy ignored him.

"But you saw what he did to poor Basil!" she protested.

"He wouldn't have done anything at all if poor Basil had left him alone," Fitzroy pointed out fairly. "The trouble came when Crawton grabbed him."

Seeing that she was making no progress, Delight shifted her ground. "The problem is that they don't keep the animal properly put away," she complained. "If Violet were to see to the matter as she should, the rest of us would not have to be troubled by it."

Halliday looked down at her, frowning. "Why do you think Miss Leigh should see to Jocko? Does the monkey not belong to her brother?"

"Oh, Adrian!" she lifted one shoulder petulantly, dismissing him with a gesture. "Everyone knows that Adrian can't be trusted to take care of anything! It is Violet who must look after their affairs."

"What about their mother?" Mr. Halliday inquired curiously. "If you choose to place the blame on someone other than Adrian, why not upon Mrs. Leigh instead of her daughter?"

"Because she never pays any attention to such things," responded Delight. "She just smiles in a perfectly lovely way and ignores them."

There was a moment's silence as they considered this, then Delight suddenly added, "Poor Violet."

Halliday looked at her in surprise, thinking that she was about to reveal her kinder nature. "Why 'poor Violet'?"

"Well, it is as plain as a gnat's eyelash that she wants Jocko present because he calls attention to her. Poor girl! She has nothing else to attract others, so she must encourage her brother's pet to misbehave so that she can be noticed."

Fitzroy's chin sagged. "Just how do you believe Jocko helped her to be noticed, Miss Ashton?"

"Why, she is the one who went to attend to Basil after the monkey had attacked him, is she not?" Delight replied, speaking slowly as though explaining something to the feebleminded.

Here she glanced about them and lowered her voice. "And she took advantage of that occasion to go *alone* into Basil's room!" she added, sighing heavily. "It is always such a pity when a young woman throws herself at a man without a thought to her reputation."

"To be honest, Miss Ashton, I cannot imagine

Miss Leigh throwing herself at anyone," said Mr. Halliday, his tone deliberate. "She might, it is true, throw some*thing* at someone—but not herself. I believe you must have misunderstood the situation."

"I assure you that I had it on the best authority," said Delight, stiff with indignation at this doubting of her account. "The maid who carried up his tray told me that Violet took the tray and went into his room *by herself.*"

"To look after him, not to throw herself at him," said Halliday. "I wonder, Miss Ashton, that you, who have known Miss Leigh all of your life, should have difficulty understanding that when I, who have known her for a much briefer period, understand it very well."

"What you do not understand, sir, being a man, is that Violet has never had the sort of natural attraction for men that many young women have."

Fitzroy, watching it all in amazement, was surprised only by the fact that she did not immediately place herself in the group with those whose natural attractions drew men like a flower draws bees.

"It has not seemed to me that Miss Leigh is lacking in attention," Fitzroy observed. "In fact, the few times I have been in contact with the lady, she has had a number of gentlemen in attendance."

Halliday looked across the room where Violet stood now with Arthur Randall and Terence Agnew. "I think you need not worry any longer about Miss Leigh," he said dryly, knowing very well that she never had. "She does very well, I think."

Delight swallowed her annoyance, wise enough to know she had gone too far, and placed her hand upon his arm. "Are you not looking forward to New

Year's Eve, Mr. Halliday?" she inquired sweetly. "I know that I am. Wassailing the apple trees is a delightful tradition."

Mr. Fitzroy looked puzzled. "I know that there is an evening party here that night—and I am familiar with wassailing. But how do apple trees fit into it all?"

"Ah, you will see, Mr. Fitzroy," replied Delight, glancing up at Mr. Halliday to be certain he was listening to her.

"Wassailing the apple trees," mused Fitzroy, who made his way over to Miss Thaxton to escort her to dinner and to hear more about this New Year's Eve activity that lay in store for them.

It was at dinner that Lord Crawton first heard of *The Lover's Vengeance*, and said that he regretted having missed the casting.

"For after all," he said, his dark eyes sliding around the group, "as an experienced lover, I feel that I could contribute my poor mite to the undertaking."

No one, even his cousin, appeared particularly taken with his observation. There was a momentary lull in the conversation, but it disappeared almost immediately as others hastened into speech.

Violet noticed uncomfortably that Crawton's eyes rested upon her rather more often than they needed to, but she refused to acknowledge him, concentrating her attention on those about her. She found herself wishing that Jocko had bitten him somewhat harder—perhaps enough to convince him to stay in his chamber the whole of the holiday.

When the gentlemen joined the ladies in the

drawing room after dinner, Lord Crawton made a point of seeking her out.

"Would you like to examine my wound, Miss Leigh?" he inquired. "Perhaps to admire the monkey's handiwork?"

"No, I would not, Lord Crawton," she said briskly. "I assure you, you dwell too much upon it."

"Yes, my valet agrees that you might have emphasized some of the dangers so strongly so that I became too conscious of them. Otherwise, I might have come downstairs long ago." He looked at her speculatively.

"I am certain that the rest did you good," she responded. "And I think you would be wise to continue to rest more than usual in order to avoid any complications."

"Yes, I am quite certain that you would like that, Miss Leigh," he said, smiling at her.

He had, she saw immediately, far too many gleaming white teeth. One mouth should not be able to accommodate them.

He took her hand before she could stop him and lifted it to his lips. "I find you most intriguing, Miss Leigh. I look forward to coming to know you better."

Mr. Randall approached just then, and Crawton bowed to her briefly and departed. She could scarcely repress the shudder that shook her. What a perfectly ghastly man, she thought. And there was still another se'nnight of his company left to endure.

On the other side of the room, Delight had noticed this byplay and had put her hand on Mr.

Halliday's arm and nodded meaningfully in Violet's direction.

"Do you see what I was speaking of?" she said in a low voice.

Halliday, seeing Randall approach Miss Leigh and Crawton depart, did not reply, turning instead to speak with Fitzroy and Miss Thaxton.

Miss Thaxton, he had been pleased to discover, was an intelligent, amiable lady, and Fitzroy appeared to enjoy her company. Considering the fastidious tastes of his friend, that was a compliment indeed. Miss Thaxton, although far from fashionable, was always dressed in a plain, pleasing manner, well suited to her spare figure and rather plain countenance. Although it was amazing, he thought, what a pair of fine, intelligent eyes did for a woman's face. His thoughts wandered briefly to Miss Leigh at this point, but he brought them to heel and back to Miss Thaxton and his present company.

After a little while, a few of the ladies played and sang, Delight leading the way, followed by Mrs. Haynes and Miss Langley. Cynthia laughingly declined, and Violet said that they had heard too much of her already, since she had played for all their dancing. Delight had inveigled Adrian into giving her a song to sing in the play, and he had done so reluctantly. He knew that if he did not, they would all be treated to tears and a fit of the dismals that would last until she finally had her way. To save time and suffering, he had put the song in immediately. Now, however, he began to feel that he would hear it in his sleep forever, for she sang it at every opportunity.

Fortunately, coffee was served before Delight had an opportunity to return to the pianoforte, and the company settled comfortably for a little conversation and a game of charades before going up for the night.

Violet had enjoyed the game, and she had talked with Mr. Randall and Mr. Agnew for a little while longer after that, watching her mother and Mr. Chesterton establish themselves to play a quiet game of casino. By the time most of the others were preparing to take their candles and go up to bed, she had grown quite mellow and relaxed.

Then, however, she realized that Adrian was no longer present. Nor were several of the other gentlemen, including Mr. Halliday and Lord Crawton.

She knew precisely where they had gone. They were gathered in the library for another late night of cards—but this time, Lord Crawton would be there.

Violet's peace of mind disappeared like a morning mist meeting the sun. There was nothing she could do, of course. If she were to call her brother out of the game, he would be humiliated and never forgive her.

As she went up to bed, she reflected again that this was an extraordinarily long fortnight. The days were passing like weeks, the weeks like months. Tomorrow would be only the sixth day of Christmas, and she and her family would not be leaving Ashton Park until after the Twelfth Day celebration.

She climbed into bed, pulled the covers over her head, and willed herself to sleep.

CHAPTER 17

Percival Fitzroy, awakening on a cot in Halliday's chamber on the morning of New Year's Eve Day, suddenly realized that he felt extraordinarily well. He lay there for a moment or two, meditating upon the wonder of that feeling. By rights, he should be miserable. He had slept on a cramped cot; he had been put out of his own room and forced to share one with Halliday; Briggs had to work in cramped conditions to effect his miracles; and he was scarcely mingling with the elite here at rural Ashton Park. In short, he had no business at all to feel so very, very well.

Nonetheless, he did.

He realized that he was humming a holiday tune after having rung for Briggs, and hurried over to the glass to see if he appeared quite himself. He peered into its depths critically. His color was good. No, his color was excellent—better than it had been in years. His eyes were bright, and it was not the brightness of fever. He hurriedly stuck out his tongue and inspected it, but it was not fuzzed or white—it, too, wore the pink of health.

As he sat down to wait for the appearance of Briggs, or that of the maid with his coffee, Fitzroy considered the strangeness of his situation. He did not consort each day with the very fashionable or the very witty—pastimes upon which he prided himself. So why should he feel so exceedingly well?

He thought for the moment of what people always said about the efficacy of country air, but he rejected that notion out of hand. He had gone on a few walks, of course—those that he could not avoid—but most of his time had been spent indoors, much of it playing cards or reading, and now, of course, rehearsing for the play. It could be the company, but then, Halliday had been his boon companion for years, and he did not recall ever feeling like this. Even granting that he was excessively glad to see Halliday safely back in England once more, his troubles apparently behind him, he could not believe that his gladness would bring about such a marked change in him.

He decided that he would consult his friend upon this interesting matter, so he marched to the bed and pulled aside its protective curtains. There was no Halliday. The counterpane was undisturbed, the pillows neatly in place. Halliday had not yet come to bed.

Fitzroy felt his sense of well-being begin to seep away from him. Since Hal had come to Ashton Park because he was considering marriage with Delight Ashton, he would scarcely be out of the room because he was occupied with another lady—and he most certainly would not be occupied with the young lady of the house, for Hal had his standards. That, Fitzroy knew, left only one option.

Hal was gambling again. Fitzroy sat down and put his head in his hands. What could he do to help this time, he wondered. He had thought that Hal was making a fresh start. Even though he was facing the loss of part of his lands once more and knew that he must marry, he obviously could do so, for Delight Ashton would accept his offer in an instant. Fitzroy had held some slight hope that he would once again offer for Miss Leigh, but he could see that there was little likelihood of that happening. He could feel the friction between them, and Miss Leigh seemed to enjoy the company of Arthur Randall. It was a pity that it must be Delight Ashton, though, and he wondered if Hal felt the same way. Perhaps that was what was driving him to gamble once more.

Hal had had some trouble just at the beginning of the holiday, but he had seemed to be doing quite well. He had not been staying up all night, and Fitzroy knew that he had been keeping the amount wagered to a minimum because of the youngsters who were playing with them. Fitzroy, although he enjoyed playing cards, had no taste for high stakes or exceedingly late hours, and he had seen no cause to sit up himself because Hal had seemed in control of himself.

But last night Crawton had been in the game again.

When the time came for the rehearsal to begin that afternoon, Adrian was not feeling well. He had not had too much to drink the night before—*well, actually*, he thought, *that would have been this morning, not last night*—but he was certainly feeling distinctly unwell. He was determined not to show it, though. It seemed very pitiful, looking as though one was still a little bit on the go at two in the afternoon.

Accordingly, Adrian took himself firmly in hand. He had no wish to think about his card playing because he knew that he had been quite spectacular in his failure. He might have won from everyone two nights ago and the night before that, but last night he had lost. There was no disguising it, no softening the blow: He had lost everything he had wagered.

He paused a moment, thinking it over. He had lost all the money he had had in his pockets, he knew that quite well. And he had lost his watch, on top of that. He tried not to consider that for the moment, because the watch had belonged to his father and neither his mother nor his sisters would be disposed to look kindly upon its loss.

For a moment Adrian buried his head in his hands. What had he been thinking? Had he been so filled with hubris that he thought that he would always win, no matter who dealt the cards and what the luck of the draw?

He shook his head. Apparently he *had* thought that, regardless of what Vi had said to him. And now here he was, wondering how he would explain to the people who meant most to him just how he had managed to get himself into this scrape.

For the watch was not all that he had lost. When he thought about the total of his losses and what he owed to the gentlemen with whom he had played, he could not even breathe. Insofar as he could see, his life was over.

However, he had his obligations to meet at the

moment. He could not fold up like a child's paper toy. He was directing the play and he would see it through to the end. He had debts of honor to pay for his losses last night, and he would somehow meet them.

For the moment, he would focus on the play.

Violet had awakened early on this morning of New Year's Eve and, feeling the bright cheer of a new beginning, she had set off for an early morning walk. On her way, however, she had passed the library and seen that her brother was just then leaving a card party. She watched from a shadowed corner as he made his way up the stairs, and she could see at a glance that he had lost. His carriage and his expression both told her as much.

Violet stood in the shadows and watched the others leave. Freddie and Beaver came out slowly, looking up the stairs after Adrian, and young Lamb and Delaney followed them, all of them looking mournful. She was not surprised, of course, to see Lord Crawton go by. She would have expected him to stay until the end and to profit by whatever mistakes the youngsters made. Then she watched Mr. Halliday walk by, and she wondered just how much Adrian had lost to him. She was distressed to realize that it mattered to her that Halliday had played cards with her brother and had undoubtedly won from him. At the very least, he had sat there and watched it happen. She found that she suddenly could not think of him without wishing him ill.

She continued outside and began her walk, not because she any longer wished to do so but because she could think of nothing else to do. She might as well be walking and worrying as sitting in her room and doing so. Perhaps, she thought, walking might clear her mind—and it was obvious that she would require an exceedingly clear mind if she were to be able to solve this problem for Adrian.

By the time she returned to the Park that morning, Violet had at least the glimmering of an idea. She had recalled something that Mrs. Ashton had told her about the evening party she had planned for New Year's Eve.

Violet smiled to herself. It was farfetched, but it might serve her purposes very well.

CHAPTER 18

Violet could not set her plan in motion immediately, but she knew that she must begin by gathering information. She knew that Adrian would be very unlikely to tell her what had happened, particularly after she had had so much to say after his last escapade at school. She knew, too, that her brothers' friends were loyal to him and would not willingly give her the details of what had happened, so she would have to select the weakest link in the chain. As soon as the opportunity presented itself—or as soon as she could make the opportunity—she would wring the information from Beaver Babcock.

Her attention was scarcely on the rehearsal that afternoon, for she was torn between watching her brother and waiting for a chance to speak to Beaver without being detected. The mood of the entire group was subdued, a fact that she laid at the door of the young gentlemen, who all looked as though they wished themselves elsewhere. Adrian, however, was gamely moving the scenes along and doing his best to appear perfectly normal.

Because she was so absorbed in other matters, Violet was caught off guard when Adrian called her name and motioned to the area they were using as a stage.

"You're on now, Vi," he called. "Where is Randall?"

Violet scanned the others in the room, but she saw no sign of Arthur Randall. He had asked her to go for a walk with him after breakfast, but she had refused, knowing that she had too much on her mind to be good company. She had not seen him since.

"I'll see if he is in the library," she said, rising and moving toward the door, but Freddie moved more quickly, informing her that he would be back in a tick. In a moment he reappeared, shaking his head.

"Not a sign of him," he informed them.

Adrian looked perplexed for a moment, then said briskly, "Well, come along anyway, Vi. We'll just have someone else read Randall's part until he gets here."

Before he could select a stand-in, Lord Crawton spoke from the back of the room.

"I would be delighted to take Randall's place," he said smoothly, threading his way through the others. "After all, I did miss the casting and this would give me just a *taste* of the play."

His eyes lingered on Violet and once again she felt her skin crawl. By now it had become her standard response to Crawton.

Adrian watched helplessly as he approached, and Cynthia looked at her sister sympathetically. It was Mr. Halliday, however, who took action.

Before Lord Crawton could reach the stage, Halliday had already slipped in place beside Violet.

"I am afraid that I have the earlier claim, Crawton," he said, smiling at Violet, who was looking at him much as someone bobbing helplessly in the sea looks at a life preserver.

"What claim would that be, Halliday?" he demanded, his dark brows almost meeting above his scowling eyes.

"Why, the right of a longer acquaintance, naturally," Halliday said easily. He looked at Violet, still smiling. "And it will give me the opportunity to play something other than a villain."

Then he turned to Adrian, ignoring Crawton completely. "I believe that Randall stands just here as the scene opens, does he not?"

Adrian assured him gratefully that he was in precisely the right place and the scene moved smoothly on its way. Violet did quite well with remembering her own lines, but she was astonished to see that Mr. Halliday knew almost all of Mr. Randall's. Miss Thaxton, who was acting as the prompter for the scene, scarcely had to help him at all. It was all the more amazing, she reflected, because his character did not appear in the scene. He had learned the lines simply because he had been watching attentively.

She realized suddenly that they had come almost to the end of the scene, the time for Mr. Randall to embrace her. It was a quick and gentle embrace, but an embrace nonetheless. Her breathing became a little quicker, and she hoped earnestly that she was not about to make a spectacle of herself. Over Mr. Halliday's shoulder she could see Delight watching her every move with narrowed eyes. She would like nothing better than to see Violet embarrass herself completely.

The embrace, when it came, seemed quite the most natural thing in the world. Mr. Halliday folded her firmly into his arms, his dark eyes merry as they met hers. Then his smooth cheek was pressed against hers and his breath caused a tendril of hair by her ear to move softly.

"I do not seem so great a villain now, do I?" he whispered.

Violet had relaxed in his arms, though her breathing was still rapid and she feared her face was flushed. When she opened her eyes, she could see that Delight's face was also flushed and her breath was most certainly coming rapidly.

The sight of Delight's distress was not what upset Violet, however. His words suddenly brought Adrian's predicament back to her with a rush, and the brief magic of the moment was gone. She stiffened and pulled away from him, ignoring his inquiring expression and the admiring murmurs of the onlookers, who thought the scene well acted.

"He plays the part better than Mr. Randall, and he's *just* the proper height for you," Cynthia told her sister approvingly.

Violet did not respond, for her thoughts had turned once more to Beaver Babcock and the problem at hand. She caught sight of him tucked away in a corner of the room, studying diligently the four lines that he needed to memorize for his part as a footman who announces the murder of the villainous uncle.

"It's quite an important part, even though it's so short," he told her anxiously. "I shouldn't wish to make a cake of myself by saying them wrong and throwing the whole play off."

"Of course you will not," Violet assured him. "I will help you with them."

Pitifully grateful, Beaver allowed himself to be guided to a corner of the almost-deserted drawing room where, Violet informed him, they would not be disturbed and he would be able to practice more readily.

By the time he had conned his lines adequately and was prepared to return to the group to deliver them, Violet had done her work. She had managed to elicit enough information about the night's play to realize that Adrian's problem amounted to more than just being badly dipped. He had pledged the income he would receive until he came of age and the major portion of what he would receive at that time. The legality of any such agreement on the part of a minor did not matter a whit, she realized, because Adrian had given his word, and he would not renege. A gentleman simply did not do such a thing. He would never be able to hold up his head again.

Even though Violet thought such an attitude foolish beyond permission, she knew that her reaction did not matter. Much as he loved her, Adrian's code was that of the other men of the *ton*, and he would live by it. Any solution she could devise would have to leave his honor intact; moreover, the world at large could not know that his problem had been solved by his older sister.

Of course, she had not the slightest notion whether her idea would work for a problem of this magnitude, but she had no choice.

She had to attempt it. If she thought hard

enough, surely she would be able to conjure up an effective plan of action.

Nothing definitive had come to her by the time they sat down to dinner that evening, but her mind was whirling. Something, she felt certain, must emerge from so much frantic activity. Mr. Randall had finally put in an appearance, abjectly apologetic about his absence during rehearsal. His walk had taken him farther afield than he had planned and he admitted, rather shamefaced, that he had gotten lost. Only the help of a passing farmer had set him back on the proper path.

He was doubly attentive at dinner as though to make up for his earlier neglect, but Violet could scarcely take note of this, let alone enjoy it. She knew that she was participating in conversations and eating her dinner, but she felt very far removed from all of it, as though she were outside the house and watching it all take place through one of the windows. Not even Delight's barbs could penetrate fully, although she was aware they were being delivered. She had not taken kindly to Mr. Halliday stepping into Randall's role that afternoon, and she had every intention of punishing Violet, once she could determine the most effective manner to do so.

Other guests were coming after dinner to attend the wassailing of the apple trees and an evening party afterwards. Violet was very glad that they were all going outside; she hoped that the crisp air might help her thinking, and she needed all the help available to her.

However, despite her preoccupation with Adrian's difficulty, the wassailing that evening almost managed to put her scheme from her mind. Like the other ladies, she had changed from her slippers to sturdy boots and put on a warm cape, and they had all walked to the apple orchard. In the meadow next to it, a huge bonfire had been built, and a group of local folk with their children were already singing.

The first song that she heard was the old, familiar one, its strains floating toward her on the frosty air.

Here we come a-wassailing
Among the leaves so green,
Here we come a-wand'ring,
So fair to be seen.

Love and joy come to you,
And to you your wassail too,
And God bless you and send you a happy new year,
And God send you a happy new year.

Mr. Ashton, she knew, was very fond of what he called "the old ways," and his wife had explained to their guests that only a few places still wassailed the apple trees, that is, still sang to them and drank to their health.

"The people used to believe that doing so would chase away evil spirits and bring a blessing on the apple trees and a good crop for the farmer," she had explained placidly. "There is nothing to it, of course, but people enjoy it."

Violet could see why they did. There was something magical about the night and the flickering fire. Next to it, a table had been set up and decorated with greenery and apples and bright ribbons. On it sat a large bowl made of applewood and filled with a steaming drink called Lamb's Wool—a hot spiced ale with roasted crab apples bobbing on its surface.

When everyone had gathered around the largest of the trees, the singing began again. This time Violet did not know the words, although she caught the first of them. *Old apple tree, we wassail thee, and hoping thou wilt bear* . . . .

After that, she lost the individual words, but understood clearly their purpose. The people were singing to the health of the apple tree, hoping that it would bear many apples that year, and at the close of the song, they cheered for it. All of the guests joined in with the cheering, understanding that part readily enough.

Mr. Ashton took a cup of Lamb's Wool and poured a libation at the foot of the tree, then raised his cup toward its branches, inviting everyone to join him in a toast.

"To your health and long life," he said, "and may my grandchildren and their grandchildren dine upon your fruit."

Delight attempted to look prettily unconscious of this reference to her own children, and glanced sidewise at Mr. Halliday as everyone pledged the tree and drank. Mr. Halliday, however, was looking in quite the wrong direction—not at Delight, not at her father nor the apple tree, but at Violet Leigh.

The roasted crab apples were not the only things bubbling and simmering in the orchard that night.

Delight was not a happy woman, and she did not intend to be unhappy alone.

A footman passed among the guests, carrying a plate of toast, and everyone was invited to take a piece, dip it into the ale, and place the toast on the limbs of the tree or around its base.

"It's a tribute to the tree, of course," Mr. Ashton explained, "but the toast is for the robins, too, that help to take care of it and make their nests there."

When the last bit of toast was tucked next to the tree, the children in the group took out tin pans and spoons and set up an unholy din, shouting as they beat on the pans.

"And that is to awaken the spirit of the tree and to keep him on guard to protect it," yelled Ashton above the racket.

"Well, if that doesn't waken him, nothing in this life will," Mr. Fitzroy informed Miss Thaxton as they left the melee behind and headed back toward the house. "I've never seen or heard anything quite like that."

"Did you not enjoy it?" she asked, looking at him anxiously.

He thought the matter over for a moment, then replied with some surprise. "Why, yes, as a matter of fact, I did. I should not mind doing it again next year."

Shocked by this admission, he absentmindedly tucked her arm through his and they walked the rest of the way in comfortable silence. Before meeting Miss Thaxton, he had not been aware that such a silence was possible with a woman. In fact, the only person with whom he had ever been upon such easy terms was Hal.

Violet's thoughts were far less peaceful, but she had at least decided upon her first steps of action. She would begin that very evening.

CHAPTER 19

As she had been certain he would, Lord Crawton bore down upon Violet as soon as they gathered once more in the house and the music began for the evening party.

"May I have the pleasure of this dance, Miss Leigh?" he asked, bowing deeply.

Mr. Randall stood beside her, and they had been talking as Lord Crawton crossed the room toward them. Violet had watched his approach from the corner of her eye. She knew that, though Mr. Randall had not asked for the first dance in so many words, he had been expecting to be her partner for it. They had been talking to pass the time until the set formed. Now, however, she had no choice but to hurt his feelings.

She gave him an apologetic glance, curtseyed to Lord Crawton, and took his arm. She tried not to see Mr. Randall's hurt expression or Mr. Halliday's startled one as her partner led her to their place.

"You will forgive my bluntness, Miss Leigh, if I tell you I am surprised at your acceptance," he said, looking at her keenly. "I was quite certain you had taken me in dislike."

Violet had no ability to evade a remark she did

not wish to respond to with a maidenly blush or a giggle, so she merely smiled and said, "And your bluntness surprises me, Lord Crawton."

"Does it indeed?" he asked, sounding completely unconvinced. "Why is it that I feel you are not easily surprised, ma'am?"

The figures of the dance moved them apart, and Violet was grateful that she need not answer him and that she need not link her arm through his nor, for the moment at least, take his hand. It required every ounce of willpower she possessed not to shudder at his touch. She would have to be watchful, though, because he was already suspicious of her sudden change toward him. Whatever else he might be, Lord Crawton was no dullard.

She rejoined her partner and, as they passed Delight and Mr. Halliday, Delight gave her the opening she had hoped for.

"Why, Violet! We had thought that we would soon be wishing you happy, but I see that Mr. Randall has found another interest." She smiled sweetly and glanced toward Mr. Randall and Miss Langley.

Fortunately, they moved on past the other couple so that Violet had no need to reply, but Lord Crawton looked at her with interest. "Since I have begun by being blunt, Miss Leigh, perhaps it is best that I continue so. It appears that my cousin does not like you greatly."

Violet shrugged. "No, she does not. Delight has never liked me. In fact, she has always done everything she could think of to make me unhappy."

His brows lifted as he watched Violet, who allowed her face to droop with discontent.

"Has she indeed?" he responded. "And how do

you feel about such Turkish treatment, Miss Leigh?"

Violet returned his gaze directly. "As though I should finally like to teach her a lesson, Lord Crawton."

Her voice was even, but she managed to inject it with some bitterness. "I have been patient with her all my life, but I have finally grown weary of having her always cast up to me my appearance and my lack of suitors."

"You will forgive me, I hope, if I say that your looks, while they are not in the common style, are quite striking, ma'am."

Violet inclined her head graciously at his compliment.

"And you do not appear to me to lack gentlemen who show an interest in you," he continued. "There is Mr. Randall, of course, from whose very arms I have wrested you, and Mr. Halliday, from whose arms I should have *liked* to wrest you this afternoon. Why should my cousin make such comments about you when they are untrue?"

"Perhaps because she is dainty and pretty and accustomed to being admired."

He cocked his head knowingly at what she had not said. "And perhaps you have *not* been always admired as you are now, and she does not like the change?"

Violet smiled. He was very quick, which would make him dangerous, but his quickness would also make her work much easier.

He accepted her smile as a confirmation, and asked another question, his tone very thoughtful.

"And just *how* would you choose to teach her a lesson, Miss Leigh?"

"By showing her that I am capable of attracting a suitor whose consequence she respects, so that at last she will have to admit my worth," replied Violet, almost holding her breath as she waited for his reply.

"Now I begin to understand the reason for your sudden kindness to me, ma'am. I had thought it for quite another reason, but I see that I was mistaken."

Violet managed to look suitably puzzled. "For what other reason, Lord Crawton?"

He shook his head. "There is no need to speak of it since I was incorrect."

He smiled once more, showing all of his teeth and putting Violet in mind of a stuffed crocodile she had seen at a friend's home. Mrs. Layton had developed an intense fondness for all things Egyptian, and she had gotten a little too carried away while redecorating her home.

"I would be more than pleased to help you in your undertaking, Miss Leigh. I find it delightful that you are so much less virtuous than you appear. It almost restores my faith in humanity."

Violet forced herself to smile. Things were, after all, going much better than she had hoped for, so she could not allow herself to feel unhappy. She was doing this, she reminded herself, for the sake of Adrian and his future, not for her own pleasure.

She spent the next dance reassuring Mr. Randall that she had not cut him because she was angry with him for having missed the rehearsal that afternoon. She soothed his ruffled feelings as well as she could, but when he discovered that she had promised to have supper with Lord Crawton, all her work was undone in an instant.

"I hesitate to say this to you, Miss Leigh," he said, his voice grave, "for no gentleman should speak ill of another. Nevertheless—"

"Please, Mr. Randall, don't say any more," she returned. "I appreciate your concern, sir, but I assure you that I am very much aware of my actions and their consequences. Pray don't feel that you must warn me or protect me."

He bowed to her very stiffly and moved away. Violet was sad, for she had not wished to distress him, but she was not grieved for any other reason. She knew that he would not ask her to dance again, tonight or any other night, and that their friendly conversations were at an end. She had disappointed him, and shown herself to be less a lady than he had thought her.

It seemed to her that she should mind more than she did, but she really had very little time to consider the matter, for she had work to do. She danced the next cotillion with Freddie, who made polished and very polite conversation with her, carefully avoiding all reference to Adrian. Since she already had the information she needed, she did not press him at all, and he made his bow at the end of the set with great relief.

A small booth had been set up at one end of the room, and within it was a dark-haired woman who professed to be a gypsy, and who also professed to be able to see the future. Mrs. Ashton had invited her to the party to provide amusement for her guests, and they appeared to be getting her money's worth, for those that gathered there seemed greatly given to laughter.

"Shall we visit the fortuneteller?" Lord Crawton inquired when he came to reclaim her for another dance.

"Of course," said Violet. "I should be delighted to know what my future holds."

The fortuneteller had Violet remove her glove and then took her right hand and studied her palm intently before looking up at her. For a moment Violet was taken aback by the expression in her huge dark eyes. She could not tell whether the expression was sympathy, understanding, or even amusement.

"You will marry soon, mistress," she said in a throaty voice, and the crowd around the booth drew in an appreciative breath. "You will marry a man who is tall and dark-haired—a wealthy man."

There was laughter from the onlookers and a couple of comments to Lord Crawton, who suited the description exactly. Of course, she thought, looking at the group around the booth, the description suited more than Crawton. There were several others, including Mr. Halliday, who matched it.

The gypsy was looking now at Lord Crawton's palm. She glanced up at him quickly, then back down at his palm, avoiding his eyes.

"Well, what do you see?" he asked crossly. "Shall I marry a tall woman with dark hair?"

There was more laughter at this witticism, but the gypsy did not smile. She shook her head.

"You will not marry," she replied, her voice low and intent.

He stared at her, startled by her tone and her words.

"What do you see?" he asked again, thrusting his palm back in front of her eyes.

Once more she shook her head. "I cannot tell you," she said. "But you would be wise to put all your affairs in order."

An abrupt silence fell at this remark, and everyone stood perfectly still as the gypsy left the booth and walked out the door.

Lord Crawton looked as though someone had transfixed him. He stood very still for a moment, then Violet took his arm.

"Let's go and have something to drink," she said in a low voice. "You will feel better then."

A low murmuring followed them, and Lord Crawton became aware, after a few minutes, that he was being constantly watched. The news of the gypsy's prediction had spread through the room like wildfire, and he was now the main focus of interest.

"What do they expect me to do? Fall over in a heap and die?" he said to Violet, turning away from all the watching eyes.

Violet shook her head. "People are just superstitious, that's all. Her prediction will be a nine-days' wonder and then everyone will forget all about it."

"Unless I happen to stick my spoon in the wall during that time," he answered dryly.

"Nonsense!" she replied briskly. "You know that she only did it for the sake of making a sensation. Any self-respecting fortuneteller knows that she must be dramatic."

"I could have done with a little less drama, I believe."

She laughed. "Come along, Lord Crawton. They are serving supper now, so let us go in. You will feel much more yourself after you have dined."

Crawton allowed himself to be led into the dining room, deeply appreciative of her support.

Violet smiled to herself. It was going to be easier than she had dared to hope.

CHAPTER 20

The evening party stretched into the early morning hours and, to her great relief, Violet saw that Adrian went directly up to bed afterwards. Lord Crawton did the same—in fact, he went to bed rather earlier—the encounter with the gypsy having apparently had much the same effect upon him as the episode with Jocko.

No one stirred early on New Year's Day and, once the company had risen, the day seemed to go as slowly as though everyone were moving through molasses. There was no rehearsal that day, and there seemed to be little heart for games or dancing. A billiards game was begun, but never ended, its participants drifting out before taking their turns. Even talk of the wassailing and the party was desultory, for no one seemed to have the heart even for gossip.

On the whole, however, Violet was pleased with the day. Nothing of consequence happened that she had to worry about, and Adrian had obviously taken his problem to heart. Although he was doing his best to wear a cheerful facade, she had no trouble seeing through it, and she was satisfied to know that his behavior was causing him to think about his actions very seriously. If she could extricate him from his present problem, she had some hope that he might mend his ways.

In a very mild spurt of afternoon activity, an attempt, Violet thought, to enliven their day, Mrs. Ashton came in to the drawing room with a large bowl of apples and a paring knife.

"What you are to do," she explained to Cynthia and Miss Langley, who were the only ones paying any serious attention to her, "is to peel your apple so that you have as long a peel as you can manage. Then you toss it over your left shoulder and look to see what shape it has fallen into. Once you see the letter that it represents, you know the first letter of the name of your true love."

The two young ladies received her instructions with enthusiasm, and they proceeded to collect a group to undergo the experiment. Although people like Mrs. Haynes had already chosen their husbands, others received the news of the game with pleasure, and a New Year's Day activity had been decided upon.

Violet watched with amusement as the girls tried it, patiently peeling an apple until they could manage a peel of respectable length, the young men calling out the letter that each toss of the apple peel appeared to represent. Once a letter had been identified, the group suggested name after name that it might represent.

After Cynthia's first toss, Beaver called out, "It's an *A*, Miss Leigh!"

"For Andrew!" suggested her brother. "Or Augustan! Or, Cyn, there's Avery! Avery Wingman!"

"You must have windmills in your head, Adrian!"

his sister responded crossly. "Avery Wingman is old enough to be my grandfather!"

She turned to look more closely at the peeling and together she and Miss Langley began to guess at other letters it might be. The trick, Violet could see, was to convince yourself and everyone else that it was the letter you wished it to be. It was not long before the *A* became an *O* and, after a few more minutes deliberation, it was determined that Cynthia should try it one more time to be certain.

This time, to Violet's interest, Freddie Tilton determined that it was an *F* and a shout went up from the others.

"Frederick!" called out Mr. Lamb amid the laughter, while both interested parties looked self-conscious, and Violet began to think that matters were becoming rather too particular. She did not have to interfere, however, for William Delaney called out that *he* thought the letter was a *W*. He was shouted down and pelted with apple peels, however, so he gave up his suit soon enough.

Mrs. Leigh watched all of this bustle affectionately from the safety of the other end of the room, where she and Mr. Chesterton were playing cribbage. When Adrian called to her to come and have a turn, she laughingly refused, answering that she was well past that sort of thing and that she would soon be wearing a cap and sitting all day by the fire.

This brought a shout of protest from the others, and she was hurried from Mr. Chesterton and the cribbage board to peel an apple of her own.

"It's an *O!* Orville!" called Freddie Tilton after she had tossed the peel over her shoulder and turned to look at it.

"Or perhaps it's Orrington!" called her feckless son, referring to a graybeard who had long admired Mrs. Leigh.

Laughing, she escaped them and returned to the safety of the cribbage board.

Some of the gentlemen strolled in from the library just then, Mr. Halliday and Mr. Fitzroy among them, and Delight rose from the group of ladies and announced that she would have her turn now. After three attempts to peel a curl of apple skin that would be suitably long—long enough to form an *H*, Violet was certain—she finally managed one. Then she tossed it and turned quickly to look at it.

"I believe it's an *L!*" called Beaver, turning to Nathan Lamb and pushing him towards Delight. "It must be Lamb you're meant to marry, Miss Ashton!"

Delight, who cared nothing at all for Nathan Lamb, argued that it did not look to her at all like an *L*, prettily requesting Mr. Halliday to come and mediate the matter.

Mr. Halliday declined that honor, declaring that he planned to keep to the safety of the other side of the room, and Delight was denied her quarry. Disconsolately, she picked up a copy of *La Belle Assemblée,* and sat turning its pages in a very deliberate manner, as though to show the others just what she thought of such a frivolous and foolish pastime.

Violet had thought to escape a turn, for she had taken out a book and attempted to arrange herself in a safe corner, but soon they set upon her as well. She peeled the apple carefully until she had a long curl, then followed Cynthia's careful instructions as she tossed it over her left shoulder.

There was another shout as it went up, but a silence fell almost immediately. Violet turned to see what had happened, and there lay her peel on the carpet, forming a precise red *C*.

Adrian recovered first and said hurriedly, "So who is it to be, Vi? Charles? Cyrano?"

"What about Carlton?" volunteered Freddie helpfully.

"Or Crawton?" inquired Delight sweetly, for she had not missed anything, despite her turning of pages.

Another brief silence ensued, and a pall fell over the game. There was a half-hearted attempt to go on with it, for Adrian pressed Freddie into trying his luck. All the younger gentleman took a turn at tossing a peel to determine their future wives, but no one appeared to have much heart for it, so the activity soon dwindled and died.

The rest of the day passed quietly, and the company went early to bed. It was peculiar, Violet thought, that the gypsy's prediction had never once been mentioned within her hearing, and that it seemed to have had such a lowering effect upon the entire group. The young men, of course, carried the heavy knowledge of Adrian's gambling debts, so she could understand their preoccupation and their transfer of it to Cynthia and Miss Langley. But it appeared that everyone had been affected—yet no one mentioned it.

As Violet prepared for bed, she reviewed the events of New Year's Eve. She felt a twinge of guilt when she thought of Lord Crawton's reaction to the prediction. He had not been seen all day, and it had been very clear to her that he had taken it to heart.

She sternly repressed a rising tide of guilty feelings, however, reminding herself of what he had done to Adrian. For several days before the party on New Year's Eve, Mrs. Ashton had talked proudly of the gypsy fortuneteller who would be there. She had been pleased that she could offer a different sort of amusement that the young people would enjoy. It had been no trick at all for Violet to approach the gypsy privately at the beginning of the evening and arrange for her to make the ominous prediction to Lord Crawton when Violet appeared at the booth with him.

She had been certain that the experience would at least provide her a starting point for her plan, but she had not imagined that it would work so well. She hardened her heart against the man's fears. He would not have to suffer long, for she hoped to have the matter taken care of very soon. In the meantime, he was safely out of the way and not engaging Adrian or any of the other young men in gambling.

Gaining his confidence so that she could guide him to the gypsy's booth had been child's play. She had known that he would believe that she was unhappy with Delight and wished to punish her, for she could see that his own mind worked in such a manner. It had also been easy to see that his inflated sense of his own worth would cause him to believe that she would see him as a means to punishing Delight. His own interest in Violet, she knew very well, had arisen primarily from her lack of interest in him. She provided him with an amusement.

As to Delight . . . Violet shook her head as she thought about that young lady. Delight did not care a whit about Lord Crawton and it would not trouble her at all if he paid court to Violet. In fact, it would amuse her because Crawton was decidedly older and less attractive than Delight's own quarry, Mr. Halliday, and he also had a decidedly unenviable reputation. She would doubtless feel that Violet had found precisely the suitor that she deserved.

It was just as well for her, she reflected, that Lord Crawton's vanity prevented his recognizing this.

CHAPTER 21

The next morning, Adrian appeared at his sister's door very early, before she had even gone down to breakfast. This was most unusual behavior for him, and Violet hurried him into her chamber, fearful that he had managed to get into yet another scrape.

He pulled his chair close to her and took her hand, his face grave. "Vi," he began, then paused as though he scarcely knew how to go on. Giving himself a brief shake, he continued. "Vi, if there's something troubling you, I want you to feel that you can confide in me."

Violet stared at him. His own problem was what was troubling her, but she had no intention of telling him so just yet, so she said nothing.

"What I mean to say is—" He broke off and looked down at his hands.

His sister watched him, puzzled. Adrian never became upset; a troubled countenance was as foreign to him as a French accent would have been.

"Just what *are* you trying to tell me, Adrian?" she asked at last, when he still did not speak or look up at her.

"Dash it all, Vi! It's Delight! I know very well that

it's *her* doing!" Adrian stood up abruptly and started pacing the room, running his hands through his bright hair until it stood up wildly.

"What is her doing?" Violet asked patiently.

"Rumormongering!" he said bitterly. "She has everyone believing that you have a *tendre* for Crawton! For *Crawton*, of all people!" He hit the top of her dressing table with his fist so that all her bottles and brushes rattled alarmingly.

When Violet did not respond immediately, he turned to her. "And you did not help anything at all, Vi, by standing up with him on New Year's Eve!"

"Did you expect me to turn down his invitation to dance?" she asked. "That would scarcely have been polite of me."

"No, of course not! But you didn't have to dance with him twice or have supper with him, Vi, nor hang on his arm at the fortuneteller's booth! Everyone remarked upon the way he leaned on you when the gypsy warned him to get his affairs in order!"

"Lord Crawton was understandably upset," she replied, her voice still calm. "I was merely helping him."

"And the worst of it, Vi, is that Delight has put it about that you were seen coming out of Crawton's room." He lowered his voice as he said this, and failed to meet her eyes.

Violet colored, but she answered him evenly. "I went to his room to help him after Jocko had bitten him. You know that, Adrian. And so does Delight. There is nothing more to it than that."

He collapsed back into his chair and looked at her ruefully. "Lord, Vi, *I* know there's nothing in that malicious bit of gossip except Delight's spitefulness! And so do Cyn and Freddie and Beaver. But some of the others, like Lamb and Delaney, don't know you as well as the rest of us. They won't say anything in front of me, of course, because I would mill them down in an instant—but I can't stop what's being whispered about you . . . or what they might tell others when they leave here."

"Of course you can't, and you mustn't let it trouble you, Adrian. The gossip will die a natural death when nothing happens to fan the flame. Promise me that you won't get into a fight with anyone; you know that would not do."

"I know enough not to upset the household, Vi, but it makes me see red when someone is talking about you in such a manner!"

She smiled at him and patted his hand. "That is very kind and protective of you, Adrian, but I assure you that I need no protection."

He looked at her anxiously. "You don't really have a *tendre* for Crawton, do you, Vi? I mean, I couldn't help seeing that you have paid most particular attention to him lately."

Violet laughed. "I promise you, Adrian, that my heart is perfectly safe from Lord Crawton. You may rest easy upon that point and ignore the gossip, for it will fade away soon enough."

She did not feel that she needed to reveal anything else to him, nor to prepare him for the possibility that there might very well be more gossip added to the fire before the flames died out.

Adrian left, satisfied at least that Violet had not fallen in love with the detestable Crawton and determined to rearrange the teeth of any gentleman foolish enough to intimate that there was anything havey-cavey about her relationship with him. He felt doubly protective toward her, and he could not tell her the whole of the affair. In trying to explain the problem to her, he had not been able to add that his own dramatic gambling loss to Crawton had heightened the scandal of his sister's supposed attachment to the same gentleman.

Violet waited until later to go down to breakfast because she did not wish to find herself in a small company with either Mr. Halliday or Mr. Randall. The awkwardness she felt with both gentlemen would have quite ruined any possibility of enjoying her meal.

She was pleased to see that she had the company of very nearly a dozen people when she entered the dining room at last, and she settled herself with satisfaction. When there was a break in the conversation, she turned toward her hostess.

"Do you know, ma'am, how Lord Crawton is faring today?" she asked.

Mrs. Ashton shook her head. "I have not seen him today. He seemed sadly low yesterday, however."

"Perhaps joining us might improve his spirits." Violet had her own reasons for desiring his presence in the group once more.

"You are quite right, Violet," agreed Mrs. Ashton. "Keeping to his room will not aid his health. I shall go up to see him myself after breakfast."

William Delaney and Nathan Lamb, who were also at the table, exchanged a significant glance, but nothing more was said on the subject of Lord

Crawton. Violet's question had elicited the response she had hoped for.

Mrs. Ashton did her work well. By the time most of the guests had gathered in the drawing room, preparing for their afternoon rehearsal, Lord Crawton had been persuaded. He entered the room as many of the guests were reading the letters that had arrived for them in the morning post.

"Basil! It's good to see you," said Mr. Ashton, rising to greet his cousin. "We missed your company yesterday."

His welcome was followed by only the most perfunctory murmur of agreement from the rest of the group. He had few fans among the other guests, but they did not wish to be openly rude to their host's relative.

Violet was reading from a letter she had slipped from between the pages of her book, and those closest to her looked up when they heard her sudden cry of surprise.

"What is it, Vi?" asked Adrian. "Have you had bad news?"

"It is from Mr. Bullock," she replied, gesturing toward the letter in her lap. "He has written the most distressing news!"

"Mr. Bullock?" said her mother, glancing at Violet with a puzzled expression. "Why is Mr. Bullock writing to you, dearest?"

"To tell us that one of the monkeys that he kept with Jocko has become ill," she replied.

"But why would he write to tell you, Violet, rather than myself or Adrian?" inquired Mrs. Leigh, still troubled.

"Very likely because I was the one that took Jocko

to him when we were going to be away from London for a few days this fall and had no place to keep him," responded Violet. "You recall that he was so kind as to allow us to leave Jocko with him."

"That's neither here nor there!" interjected Adrian impatiently. "What's this about an illness?"

"It seems that one of the monkeys fell sick, and now one of the servants that took care of them has fallen ill, too. Mr. Bullock writes that what the servant has looks a great deal like cowpox, except that they call it monkeypox, of course."

Lord Crawton had grown pale. "How did the servant contract the illness, Miss Leigh?" he asked. "Does he tell you in the letter?"

She nodded gravely and paused, for dramatic effect. Lord Crawton was not the only one listening intently. "He writes that the servant was bitten."

Lord Crawton gave a low moan and rose from his chair. "I think I must go to my room," he croaked, and moved slowly toward the door.

"I think I'll just go up and have a look at Jocko," said Adrian, anxious about his pet. "I don't think he has a fever and he's been behaving normally, but I'd best go and see him."

He hurried out of the room, passing Lord Crawton on the stairs. Crawton clung to the railing and took each step individually, as though he already felt the hand of the disease upon him.

"Well, it lacked only this," said Mr. Fitzroy to Mr. Halliday. "I was beginning to feel kindly toward the monkey. He has kept to his own chamber recently, and he has attacked only the proper people. Now we must worry that we will catch some loathsome disease."

Even Mrs. Ashton and Mrs. Leigh appeared to feel that there was some reason for worry, for Mrs. Leigh thought about the matter for two whole minutes before turning to a game of whist with Mr. Chesterton, and Mrs. Ashton rang for the butler and asked him to send up a glass of brandy to Lord Crawton.

"Basil is certainly having the devil's own luck," observed Mr. Ashton before retiring to the library and the newspaper that had come with the post.

Mr. Halliday had not responded to Fitzroy's comment. He watched Miss Leigh with interest, as she folded up the letter and slipped it into her book. A minute or two after Lord Crawton crept from the room, he saw that she strolled over to the fire and casually dropped the letter into it.

Monkeypox or no monkeypox, the rehearsal began as soon as Adrian had returned from his visit upstairs.

"There is nothing amiss with Jocko!" he announced cheerfully when he reentered the drawing room. "He has no sign of a fever and he's eating well—just as full of frisk and frolic as he always is."

"I feel so much better now," murmured Fitzroy to Halliday.

"I thought of bringing him down for the rehearsal, but I decided that since we have a very great deal to do and need all our powers of concentration, I would leave him upstairs."

This drew a universal murmur of agreement. Had Adrian come in with the monkey on his shoulder, Violet felt that the chances were excellent that there would have been no rehearsal, and that all of the guests would have retired immediately to their chambers.

Adrian, happily unaware of this undercurrent and eager to focus his attention on the rehearsal so that he could forget about the problem of Lord Crawton for the moment, hurried the players to their places.

"For we must remember," he reminded them, "that we have only today and tomorrow to practice. We would not wish to disgrace Mrs. Ashton in front of her guests when we present *The Lover's Vengeance* to them."

The rest of the players seemed as eager as Adrian to give their attention to something, and they fell to rehearsing with more enthusiasm than they had shown for anything in the past few days. Concentrating on something outside themselves appeared to make all of them, except Delight, much more cheerful. The only break that they allowed themselves was for dinner, and then they practiced straight through until a late supper was served.

Once again, Violet had the satisfaction of seeing Adrian go directly to his room after supper. And she knew that Lord Crawton was still cowering in his room, waiting for any sign of monkeypox, or even the faintest sign of a fever.

Her plan was proceeding apace, and she was grateful to have it and the play to concentrate upon, for she did not wish to think of the unhappy Mr. Randall, who had retreated behind a cool, distant manner, or of the enigmatic Mr. Halliday, who appeared to be watching her every move.

CHAPTER 22

By the time the day of the performance arrived, the players felt that they had very nearly polished *The Lover's Vengeance* to perfection. They had rehearsed almost every waking hour for the two days before it, practically dropping from exhaustion by the end of each day, and Beaver complained that he heard his four lines even during his sleep. Lord Crawton and Jocko had both kept to their rooms, which the others considered a very satisfactory state of affairs.

Some twenty guests arrived on the day of the great event, and all were in a very agreeable state of excitement, pleased to have a theatrical to enliven their holiday. The players, for their part, were poised for a great success. "I daresay we'll be invited to The Theatre Royal," Freddie whispered just before the makeshift curtain rose to begin the play.

Everything went as faultlessly as is possible for such an amateur affair. There were two or three moments of anxiety: once when an ornamental tree representing a forest fell off its stand and just missed pressing the hapless Beaver into the floor, and again when the collapsible knife for the murder could not be located and Mr. Halliday feared that a real one might have to be substituted. However, all three pairs of lovers were appropriately loverlike—though Mr. Randall was even more reticent than usual—Mr. Halliday was satisfyingly villainous and Mr. Fitzroy suitably bloodthirsty in his murder of the wicked uncle (fortunately, by that time armed with the stage knife), and Beaver delivered all four of his lines perfectly, if without noticeable feeling.

At the supper afterwards, the performance was examined and discussed from every possible perspective. Those who had been members of the audience were gratifyingly complimentary, and the members of the cast modestly appreciative. Over coffee and cakes in the drawing room, the misadventures unknown to those out front were recounted. The audience learned that Mr. Tilton's ring had become tangled in Miss Langley's curls during a tender moment onstage, forcing him to improvise a sort of little dance to get them offstage so that his ring could be extricated. Although because of the tremendous crash the audience had been aware of the falling of the potted tree, they had not realized Mr. Babcock's close brush with permanent disfigurement because of it, nor had they known of Mr. Halliday's fears about a real knife in the hand of Mr. Fitzroy.

"I don't know what the problem was, Hal," Mr. Fitzroy complained after that story was recounted. "I would not have injured you and the blade would have looked much more authentic."

"I am glad that you feel so, Fitz, but somehow I had dire misgivings about your concern with authenticity leading to my very authentic death," replied Mr. Halliday placidly.

"May we discuss another subject, please?" said Lord Crawton, who had been coaxed down for the performance.

The others glanced at one another and turned the subject immediately to matters unrelated to both death and monkeys.

"Now that we have survived the play," said Cynthia, "we must get our costumes organized for the masquerade. Thank heavens that Adrian insisted upon allowing us a day between the play and the ball, or we should never be ready."

"I already have my costume prepared," remarked Delight, her air smug. "I am to be Marie Antoinette."

"Shall I bring my little guillotine?" inquired Adrian with a grin.

Delight gave an indignant sniff. "You show remarkably poor taste about a very serious matter!" she informed him. "I shall wear a red ribbon around my throat to signify her tragic death."

At this further mention of death, Lord Crawton paled and coughed alarmingly.

"What will you come as, Basil?" asked Mrs. Ashton, eager to divert his thoughts.

Lord Crawton shook his head. "I don't believe I shall attend," he said weakly. "I'm not certain, but I think that I may have a fever."

She rose and walked directly to his chair, resting her hand for a moment on his forehead. "You are perfectly cool, Basil, and it will do you good to come. Why not come as a pirate? That will be easy enough to manage."

Satisfied by his silence that she had won her point, Mrs. Ashton returned to her chair.

Mr. Fitzroy leaned quietly to Halliday and whispered, "Perhaps he can have a monkey on his shoulder rather than a parrot."

Halliday smiled at this sally. "What will your costume be, Fitz?"

"Miss Thaxton and I have not yet decided," he replied, and his friend regarded him with interest.

"You and Miss Thaxton are planning your costumes together?" he asked, a hint of laughter in his voice.

Fitzroy recognized that tone very well, and he answered with an air of injured dignity. "Yes, we thought we might very well be able to work something out together."

"I daresay you will," said Halliday, "and I am very glad to hear it."

Fitzroy did not deign to reply, devoting his attention to his coffee instead. Mr. Halliday's gaze wandered across the room, until it fell upon Violet, who was talking with Lord Crawton. He found that the sight irritated him very much, and he turned away.

When the last of the guests from afar had said their farewells and ridden away into the bright, moonlit evening, those left at Ashton Park took their candles and retired gratefully to their beds.

Or at least almost all of them did.

Downstairs in the library, a small collection of gentlemen sat down with their cards. Having missed several evenings of play, they had decided to resume their game once more.

Mr. Halliday glanced around the room. He had

convinced Adrian to make one of the party once again, and the boy had reluctantly consented, praying that tonight his luck would be in. His friends were there as well, all of them looking grim rather than festive. Indeed, Freddie Tilton had attempted to convince Adrian not to come, but Adrian had insisted.

"Don't you see, Freddie? I've got no other answer to my problem. If I win tonight, I'll be able to start making a small dent in what I owe to Crawton. I don't have any other way to pay him."

"I thought you'd lost everything, Adrian. What are you going to wager?"

Shamefaced, Adrian took out his snuffbox, an expensive gold one studded with emeralds. It had belonged to his grandfather.

Freddie shook his head sadly and followed his friend in to the table. All of Adrian's companions had the air of a group gathering for a wake.

Violet had seen them gathering. She had watched every evening, knowing that this time would roll round. Although she knew that Adrian deeply regretted his loss, she had felt certain that he would end up at the table once again, trying to recoup his losses.

She had waited for this moment.

Just before the game began, Halliday held up his hand. "Just a moment, if you please. I believe we are missing someone."

The others looked up, puzzled.

"Lord Crawton should be here," he said, and the others looked at him in dismay. "I shall go up and get him."

Before there could be an outcry against Halliday's plan, the door of the library opened and Lord Crawton strolled in. Or at least he attempted to stroll. Because of his present state of mind, his walk more closely resembled a totter.

Mr. Halliday looked at him in astonishment. "We did not expect you, Crawton. I had thought I would have to coax you to come down and join us."

Lord Crawton sank into his chair and shook his head weakly. "I heard you were playing and couldn't stay away," he croaked. "Didn't want to miss a game."

Here he pulled some things from his pocket and laid them on the table—Adrian's voucher, and the gold watch that had belonged to Violet's father.

"Here's my stake," he added. He glanced across the table at Adrian. "I thought I would give you an opportunity to win it back."

Adrian stiffened and nodded without a word. This was his chance to clear the slate and walk away, and he was determined to do so. He shook his head to clear his wits, and the gentlemen settled down to serious play.

Almost four hours later, the door to the library opened and the gentlemen walked out. Violet, who had been waiting all this while on the gallery that overlooked the entry hall, hurried down the passage to her chamber. Standing just inside it, she left the door slightly ajar so that she could watch Adrian as he passed. The candlelight flickered on his face, and she could see that he looked haggard, but elated. He walked with a spring in his steps that had been missing for the past few days, and in his hand was their father's gold watch. Behind him came his friends, joking companionably, light-hearted once more.

Violet closed the door and went gratefully to bed. Adrian was free of Lord Crawton and he had reclaimed his inheritance. Now if he could only keep himself from falling into another scrape before they left Ashton Park and got safely home, she felt that she would be eternally grateful.

CHAPTER 23

The change in Adrian and his friends was obvious to everyone the next day. Merriment was their watchword, and jokes and pranks abounded. No one was safe—except perhaps Lord Crawton, who was once more secure within his own chamber.

The next two days were given over to the planning and execution of costumes, and Mrs. Ashton opened her attics and the trunks therein to the merrymakers. Many of them had brought costumes with them, or at least bits of costumes, for a masquerade was common on Twelfth Night and they liked to be prepared. Nevertheless, rooting through the Ashton treasures in the attic was a most enjoyable way to spend a few hours.

Adrian discovered his costume almost immediately, and soon had found everything he needed to make a very passable cavalier. He took to wearing his plumed hat and sword immediately, clanking around the attic and occasionally tripping one of the others with the sword. When he disappeared into the nether regions of the attic at one point, they could hear him leaping about, practicing his fencing.

"You could profit by more practice at Angelo's!"

called Freddie. "You're more likely to hurt yourself than to win a duel!"

Adrian disregarded his friend and continued his leaping back, in his own mind a veritable paragon of all the romantic qualities of a Royalist.

Fitzroy and Miss Thaxton had settled upon being a pair of gypsies, having been greatly struck by the fortuneteller on New Year's Eve.

"But we shall not attempt to tell anyone's fortune," Fitzroy informed Mr. Halliday, "and we can only hope that if Crawton decides to come, he does not faint dead away at the sight of us."

He looked at Halliday closely for a moment. "You were playing cards again last night, weren't you, Hal?"

Halliday nodded. "And I beg you to remember, Fitz, that you are not my parent, and so you need not worry over me."

"And Crawton played?" Fitzroy persisted.

Again Halliday nodded.

Fitzroy hesitated a moment, then added reluctantly, "It might be a good thing to make that more widely known, Hal."

"To make what more widely known? That Crawton was present?"

Fitzroy nodded. "There is a rumor going about, you see. Miss Leigh was seen going into his room after everyone went up to bed last night. No one saw her come out."

"And I can imagine just where the rumor came from," said Halliday grimly. "Miss Ashton is altogether too busy about other people's business."

"Will you do anything about it?" asked Fitzroy.

"All we can do is to say what we know if the matter arises, Fitz. I can scarcely call everyone together and announce that a rumor is being spread about Miss Leigh, then tell what the rumor is and why it isn't true. That would only work up still more rumors."

He paused a moment. "And, aside from that, I am quite certain that Miss Leigh *did* go to his room—it's just that she certainly did not go for the reason that Miss Ashton implies."

Fitzroy looked shocked. "She went to his room? Why would she do such a thing?"

"That is one thing I would very much like to know," replied Halliday. "But there is one thing that I can tell you about the situation with Miss Ashton, Fitz."

"And what is that?" Fitzroy steeled himself for the news that he was about to offer for the young lady.

"I am not going to marry her. I could not endure living with someone who makes it her business to attempt to run everyone else's and to puff herself up at the expense of others."

Fitzroy let out a sigh of relief. He had not looked forward to seeing Delight Ashton on a regular basis.

"Then what will you do about the moneylender, Hal? Do you have a plan?"

Halliday shrugged. "I suppose that I shall have to work that out. At the moment, I merely know what I will *not* do."

Violet and Mr. Randall had thought of their costumes the previous week, when they were still on close terms. They had planned to go as a shepherd and shepherdess. Now, she could not decide just what she should do. To her surprise, however, Mr. Randall approached her, speaking to her in a friendly fashion for the first time since New Year's Eve.

"I thought, Miss Leigh, that since you are changing your costume, you might not mind if Miss Langley were to wear the shepherdess dress."

Violet looked at him, puzzled. "What makes you think I am changing my costume, sir?" she asked. "Is it because we have had a falling-out?"

Mr. Randall looked distressed. "No, naturally not, Miss Leigh, but I was told—that is, I thought I was told—perhaps I misunderstood."

"Pray tell me what you thought you were told, Mr. Randall, and just who did the telling."

He looked more distressed than ever. "It was Miss Ashton. She informed me that she was certain you and Lord Crawton were going to plan your costumes together."

"Did she indeed?" replied Violet grimly. "Well, we shall just see about that. In the meantime, sir, you may tell Miss Langley that she is very welcome to the shepherdess costume."

"Thank you, Miss Leigh. She'll be grateful, I am certain—but I do apologize for upsetting you. Perhaps I misunderstood Miss Ashton."

"I should imagine that you understood her very well, sir. Miss Ashton can make herself painfully clear."

Mr. Randall departed in haste, and Violet set out to find Delight. When she located her coming down from the attic, she closed in immediately.

"Delight!" she said sharply.

Her tone brought Miss Ashton up abruptly. She was not accustomed to hearing Violet speak in such a tone, but she overcame her surprise and bristled immediately.

"What do you want, Violet?" she asked lazily.

"Just what have you been telling Mr. Randall about me and my change in plan for costumes?"

They both heard steps on the stairway behind Delight and looked up. It was Mr. Halliday, who paused to see what was happening.

"Why, I merely mentioned to him that you and Lord Crawton would very likely be planning your costumes together," Delight responded, smiling sweetly.

"And why would you think such a thing?" asked Violet.

"The fact that I saw you slip into his bed chamber late last night, and I did not see you slip out again." Her smile intensified and she glanced up at Mr. Halliday to see if he was appreciating her performance.

"Why *did* you go to Crawton's chamber, Miss Leigh?" asked Halliday, shocking both of the ladies. "I am quite certain that you did—although I know that what Miss Ashton is implying is not true, because Crawton spent almost the whole of his night playing cards with me downstairs."

Once again both ladies looked shocked, though for very different reasons this time.

"How do you know that I went to his chamber if you did not see me do so?" asked Violet, turning to Mr. Halliday.

"Because he came downstairs to the game without my going up to force him to do so."

She looked at him a long moment, studying his face. "And why would you force him to do so?"

"Because he had indulged himself in a most unfortunate habit of his—commonly known as 'fuzzing the cards'—and won a most unseemly amount from one of the young men. I knew exactly how he had done it, so I had planned to reveal that to him and accompany him back downstairs so that he could restore to the young man what was properly his."

He paused in his story and looked at her. "But he came down without my urging, and deliberately allowed the young man to win back everything. Just how did you force him to do that, Miss Leigh?"

Delight had been totally forgotten in this account. Mr. Halliday and Miss Leigh were clearly aware only of one another.

"I threatened him," she answered calmly. "I told him that if he did not allow Adrian to win back what he had lost, he would find Jocko in his room with him. When he was asleep, when he was least prepared, that was when Jocko would appear. And I told him that Jocko now disliked him so intensely that there could be no doubt of the outcome. And I told him that the servant who had taken care of the monkey that was ill had died of monkeypox."

"And had he?" inquired Halliday, his lips quivering.

Violet shook her head. "Of course not. There was no servant, no sick monkey, no monkey pox. I made it all up."

Delight gasped. "Why you dreadful—"

Before she could complete her sentence, however, Mr. Halliday interrupted. "I think, Miss

Ashton, that before you speak, you should consider the advisability of forgetting everything you just heard."

Delight stared at him.

"If you don't, you see," he explained gently, "then everyone here will come to know that you have been telling tales about Miss Leigh, and that, of course, will make you appear a jealous minx."

"Jealous?" said Delight blankly. "Jealous of Violet?"

He nodded. "Rest assured I shall be certain they know it unless you cooperate, ma'am."

Bowing to both startled ladies, he went quietly on his way.

The Twelfth Night masquerade was a huge success. Spirits were high, as though after being oppressed for so many days they had broken free and sailed as high as they were able.

Violet had at last decided to go as a gypsy, too, deciding that she had much for which to be grateful to the gypsies. Furthermore, it was a simple enough costume to conjure up. As she assembled her costume, she thought of Mr. Halliday and what he had been prepared to do for Adrian. She had, she thought, misjudged him. He had indeed changed during the past two years and was clearly much more inclined to think of other people.

Her first dance that evening was with Mr. Halliday, attired as a highwayman. "I shall look forward to having you tell my fortune later, dear lady," he told her as he led her onto the floor.

She smiled. Perhaps, she thought, she might be

able to do just that. Neither she nor anyone else at Ashton Park any longer believed that he was going to offer for Delight. That had become abundantly plain, and the fact that he was not dancing the first dance with her had put a period to it all.

"Just what do you think my fortune will be?" he asked, as they came together later in the dance.

"That depends upon the answer to my question, sir," she told him gravely. "Do you still need to marry in order to gain your fortune?"

He looked at her, startled. "How do you know that, Miss Leigh?" he demanded.

She smiled. "I learned that two years ago, Mr. Halliday," she assured him.

"And you knew it when I offered for you then?" he asked, his voice flat.

She nodded, still smiling.

"How can I apologize to you for what I did?" he asked, his voice low. "I wonder that you are still dancing with me and have not simply turned and walked off the floor."

"People do occasionally change, I understand," she remarked kindly. "And you have not answered my question."

She paused looked at him. "Is your need for your fortune still as great as it was?"

He nodded.

"And is it once again an immediate need? Is that why you were about to marry once again?"

He nodded.

"Then allow me to tell your fortune, sir," she said softly, her eyes laughing. "I believe that, on the Twelfth Day of Christmas, you will become engaged to a tall, dark woman, and that you shall always celebrate that day as the beginning of your life together."

Stopping stock still in the middle of the dance, Mr. Halliday took her into his arms and kissed her tenderly.

Mr. Fitzroy and Miss Thaxton, along with all the others, stopped to watch. "Well, thank goodness, Hal!" said Fitzroy. "My friend, I wish you joy!"

Cheering and applause broke out from the gaggle, led by the astonished Adrian. Violet smiled up at her highwayman. It had been, after all, a *most* satisfying holiday.